D1627039

Mercy

A Contemporary Retelling of Ruth

S.E. Clancy

S.E. Clancy

ISBN: 978-1-7335195-1-9

Origami Crickets Publications

Cover photograph by Brett Sayles

To Dad, who stood up when it was right, even when you were standing alone. I love you.

Chapter 1

Mercy swallowed hard, peeling her lips apart. Her mouth tasted like the wrong end of a hangover. Someone patted her arm and she relaxed into the touch. Muscles screaming from sitting upright for two hours on the uncushioned bus seat the night before and the six hour plane ride before that, Mercy stretched out, feeling her toes push over the end of the sofa bed.

Her mother-in-law chuckled. "Hey." Adele continued to massage Mercy's arm through the jacket.

Mercy worked her tongue around her mouth while her eyelids cracked open, adjusting to the bright sunlight in small doses as it filtered through the thin, white curtains. "What time is it?"

She took a moment to assess the guest house. All she wanted the night before was a bed, and the sofa bed was the next best thing. There was a short, yellow kitchen counter with a half-sized oven. A compact bathroom was tucked into the back corner. Curtains on a rod from the ceiling divided off a tiny bedroom. Everything was small in the converted garage.

Adele smiled, her silver-threaded hair laying in a braid over one shoulder. "Heather woke me up a bit ago. It's lunch time."

"I feel like I just went to sleep."

"I know, kiddo. Let's go eat in the big house and get it all sorted."

The sofa springs creaked when Mercy sat up. Adele pushed the cushions to the side so they wouldn't tumble to the floor.

Running her fingers through the tangles in her hair and twisting it up into a bun, Mercy then stood and trailed Adele out of their new home, beside fresh flowers planted in colorful pots, and toward the "big house." It'd been dark when the Benson women had arrived. Now Mercy finally got her first glimpse at the two-story home with shutters and a wrap-around porch—straight out of a romance movie. The majestic mountains beyond the tree-dotted town only made Mercy wonder if Santa Claus had a part-time job here in Fayette, California.

Dr. Heather Kinnett already waited at the back door, hand resting on her pregnant belly. "Good afternoon. I hope you got a good nap." She was thirty-eight-years old, smack dab in the middle of Mercy's twenty-two and Adele's sixty-years-old, and their third cousin on the Benson side. Two weeks before, she'd offered her guest house to the women she now ushered into the kitchen.

A meaty aroma wafted passed the open doorway. Mercy's mouth flooded in hunger, and her stomach rumbled a response. She smiled nervously, relieved when Heather laughed.

A young man jostled past Mercy's elbow on his way out of the house, baseball hat in hand, and a thick slice of bread between his lips. He paused when he looked up and saw Mercy. "Excuse me ma'am." He dipped his chin down as he pulled his hat over his short dark hair.

"You're going to be late again, Robert." Heather waved as he crawled into a rusted truck in the driveway and rolled out of sight. Mercy couldn't help but notice the way he glanced back toward her, like he might call out something. Heather turned to her guests. "My brother swings by for lunch a couple of days a week.

"You probably haven't had a decent meal since you left the city." She beckoned her destitute family into the kitchen and pulled two chairs from the table for them.

Heather's remark struck closer to the truth than she knew; the pair only ate meager meals for the last month. Every penny had been spent on airfare to the West Coast, after Adele's layoff from the bank and Mercy's stint as a janitor abruptly ended. They'd opened up their eviction notice the same morning Heather had sent an email offering her guest house. She'd heard from another family member that Mercy and Adele had wanted to leave New York City.

Heather hadn't even asked the pair's reason for leaving.

The food was splayed across the table: sliced bread, steaming stew in a pot, and a bowl of dark, ripe blackberries. Mercy had only seen the expensive berries once in a store. She had been promptly chased with a baseball bat after stealing a handful.

"Are those really blackberries?" Mercy eyeballed the purple fruit.

"Yup. There are patches everywhere around here," Heather said. "We need to get busy picking to make our jams for the year. If we're lucky, we can find some leftover strawberries in the back that the deer haven't eaten."

Mercy and Adele eased down into chairs across from Heather and her twins. Jenna, a pale and petite girl, stared at Mercy until elbowed by Michael, skinny with dirt clinging to his knuckles. Jenna grabbed the ladle in the stew and filled a bowl held by her older twin brother. Michael extended the bowl toward Mercy in exchange for Mercy's empty one.

"I'll say grace and we'll dig in," Heather said.

Mercy focused on the food while Heather prayed, oblivious to the words. The brown broth, filled with chunks of carrots, meat, and potatoes demanded her attention with its delicious smell. "Amen," barely passed Heather's lips when Mercy thrust the first spoonful into her mouth.

The second and third shoveling of stew commenced in the same fashion until Mercy happened to catch movement across the table. Michael held out a piece of sliced bread.

"Thank you." Mercy washed down her hasty bites with some water. She made herself slow down. Noticing the others around the table had already done so, she pulled her napkin into her lap, feeling the heat rise in her cheeks from her lack of etiquette.

"I don't think Mercy has ever seen a blackberry patch," Adele suggested, spilling a few of the berries onto a plate between the two of them.

"Did you grow up in New York?" Jenna's tiny voice lisped, her brown eyes round.

Mercy finished the bite of bread she had dunked into the stew. "Mmm hmm." She hoped they wouldn't ask any more questions about her childhood. Fatherless, passed around from family members to friends after her mother died, and then drinking until she passed out drunk when she was fourteen were particulars Mercy would rather keep tucked into the darkest parts of her past. She comfortably sat in silence while they ate.

"We can take you to the patch at the creek after lunch," Michael said in a raspy voice, far older than an eleven-year-old should sound. Mercy eyed the boy: shaggy hair, almost black, brushed his collar. His dark brown eyes scrutinized her face when he caught her staring, eyebrows twitching down.

"Not me, I'm afraid," Adele said, laying her hand on the checkerboard tablecloth. "But, Mercy can go with you. You guys can teach her about all of the things in the country that she's never seen or heard of before." Adele leaned forward on her bony elbows and dropped her voice to an exaggerated whisper. "She's never even seen a real cow before!"

Jenna burst into a fit of petite giggles and Michael scrunched his eyebrows together.

"I've seen a picture of a real cow," Mercy said. She pushed a spoonful of stew into her mouth, eyes on her meal, unable to face another jab at her ignorance.

"We can even show you how to milk one!" Jenna wiggled from side to side in her chair. "We can show you lots of things that you prolly never learned in the city, if you want, Mercy."

"Okay. I didn't get to see much, since it was dark when we got here last night."

"We know." Michael's monotonous voice matched his flat expression. "We were awake."

"Michael Alexander Kinnett. Mind your manners." Heather glared at her oldest.

His head bowed. "Yes, ma'am."

"Okay, you two finish up and go get on your mucks and boots for picking. I'll fill up a canteen for you and get the buckets. And be quiet because your daddy is asleep." Heather sent the kids off with a flick of her wrist. Once they had scrambled from the table and pounded up the stairs, Heather turned back to her guests. "David works nights as a forest ranger. And I'm sorry about Michael. He tends to be suspicious of strangers, as we have taught him to be, but that doesn't excuse his attitude toward family."

Mercy wiped the corners of her mouth. "I am a stranger." Her fingers twitched near her empty bowl. There was plenty of stew in the pot but Mercy refused to ask for more, not wanting her stomach to reject the entire meal because she had gorged herself. Instead, she downed the last of her water.

"Do I need to wear anything special?" She rubbed her worn jeans and smoothed her wrinkled t-shirt.

"Not at all. You have boots on, so you're good to go."

Heather placed the cast iron pot onto the stove, lid firmly in place. Adele shuffled across the tiled floor, bringing the last of the bread to Heather at the kitchen counter. Not knowing what else to do, Mercy gathered the dirty bowls and deposited them into the chipped, white sink. Outside the window above the sink, brown-tipped leaves swayed in a breeze. There was not a skyscraper in sight, only trees and puffy clouds in the bluest sky Mercy had ever seen. It'd be easier to say she was tired instead of trudging outside. Far simpler to say she needed a nap so that she could cry herself to sleep in a house that wasn't even their own.

Clomping boots descended the staircase, heralding the Kinnett twins, dressed in stained pants and scuffed leather footwear. Jenna's hair had been captured into a side braid, brushing her belly button.

"Ready, Mercy?" Jenna's tiny voice whistled through her missing top teeth.

"Sure."

Heather handed over a couple of well-used plastic buckets with metal handles.

"We'll be up on Payne's Creek." Michael took the beat-up canteen from his mom, the braided rope slung diagonally across his lithe body. "Yes, I have my cell phone, a bandana in my pocket, and I'll grab the rake before we leave." He yanked the kitchen door open, nodding his head at Mercy to proceed.

"Have fun!" Adele called.

Mercy peeked over her shoulder and saw Adele giving her a tiny wave as she followed the twins out to the gravel driveway. Part of Mercy wanted to stay there, clinging to Adele, trying to make sense of the quietness in their new home. No taxi horns, no incessant white noise from bus engines, or neighbors' televisions. Only birds and a random car or truck driving somewhere nearby.

A big black cat circled Mercy's ankles before Jenna shooed it away. "Go on, Leo." She petted the cat and then pushed him toward the house. "Mom won't let us have him inside. Robert's allergic."

Michael marched passed Mercy, who stood in the gravel. "I gotta get the rake."

"What for?"

Jenna slipped her hand into Mercy's after Michael's loaded silence. "It's for rattlesnakes."

Mercy swallowed hard and her stomach rolled. She'd only ever heard about the venomous snakes and their lightning-fast strikes in Western movies. Had she really moved to a place where she could be killed in a matter of seconds from a vicious, blood-thirsty reptile? An involuntary shiver shook her body.

Jenna chattered on about Payne's Creek and the family it had been named for, hundreds of years ago. Then she switched to talking about their homeschooling, followed by Uncle Robert's ability to eat massive amounts of food. When the girl tired of those subjects, she switched to the birds she could hear and see. "That's a red-winged blackbird. And that's a crow, which is diff'rent than a raven. Did you know they are two different birds, but people get them mixed up all the time?"

Mercy listened to Jenna's verbal local library, observing the birds when prompted and keeping her eyes on the path for any slithering enemy. Trees lined both sides of the dirt path, much different than the ones back in New York—they almost looked greener here in Fayette. And the bird following them, swooping from branch to branch high above, ever changing its tunes, seemed to annoy little Jenna the most.

"That's a mockingbird," she huffed. "Dad says the males steal the songs of the other birds just so they can show off to the females. I don't know why girl birds would be impressed by that."

The air temperature dropped slightly before the smell of water filled Mercy's nose, along with something sweet. She could just make out the sound of running water behind a giant wall of green leaves. It was the biggest bush she had ever seen, well over six feet high and as wide as Heather's house.

Michael dropped the metal pronged rake to the ground, flipping the sharp side to the dirt with his boots. "Can't have anyone impaling themselves. Ma'am?" He held out a bucket for Mercy and nodded for her to take it. "You've really never seen a blackberry bush?"

Mercy remained mute. She shook her head to indicate her inexperience of the situation.

"So, come up here and let me show you the problem."

Mercy's stare flew to the ground, certain snakes would be emerging from the greenery. To the side, she saw Jenna step onto the lower branches, immersing her tiny body into the vines.

Michael chuckled. "There shouldn't be any snakes in the berries. It's too cool down here for them. You have'ta worry about thorns." He pulled Mercy closer to the blackberry patch and showed her the thorns on both the vines and the leaves. "The ones on the leaves hurt worse. They're so tiny that they break off under your skin, so take your time. We'll have a full bucket in an hour or so."

"Can I eat one?"

Jenna giggled from somewhere in the brutal vines. "Yes. Just don't eat too much. You'll get a stomach ache."

Mimicking Michael beside her, Mercy tromped on the lower vines to access the dark berries farther into the patch. Her jeans caught on some thorns.

"Pull up on the leaves when they catch." Michael showed her the motions as his own denim snagged. "If you pull too hard, you'll rip your pants. That's why Mom makes us wear our work clothes for this."

"Is it ripe if it's black?"

"Pretty much. A little bit of pink will make it sour. But no green. Here's some good ones for you to eat." Michael reached across the gap between their bodies and deposited two plump berries into Mercy's hand.

"Thank you." Mercy popped the first berry into her mouth and let it sit on her tongue, playing with the bumpy surface as it rolled around. She smashed it into the roof of her mouth and was rewarded with a delicious sweetness. She hummed and swallowed. The second berry quickly followed the first.

"Jenna and I can make a cobbler for dessert tonight." Michael pushed the bucket into a blank space in the vines and deposited berries by the handful. "We usually do that with fresh berries the first night." He smiled at Mercy before ducking back into his work area.

Mercy watched as the younger boy worked his hands into crevices, avoiding the thorns, returning with enormous amounts of fruit. Michael calculated where he placed his feet and stepped deeper into the bush.

"Waddly-ah-chee-dah, waddly-ah-chee-dah, doodally-do, doodally-do." Jenna's voice sang in tune with the red-winged blackbird that hopped from branch to branch, high above their heads.

"Did those tattoos hurt when you got them?"

Mercy turned to see Michael gazing at her right arm, where the overlapping designs nearly covered every inch of skin. His eyes flicked up to her neck. To the black lotus blossom creeping above her collar. "Sometimes."

Jenna emerged from the greenery. "Why'd you get them?"

Mercy traced a finger along the mandala on her wrist. "My husband got some, so I did too."

"Did you guys get matching ones?" Michael asked.

"No. He got different ones." She missed her name carved onto Derrick's bicep.

"Do you have any pictures of his?" Jenna started to move closer.

"No."

Jenna stopped within a couple of feet. "Why not?"

Mercy swallowed hard and rubbed the clutch of feathers tattooed at her elbow. "He died and my phone with all of his pictures was stolen."

"Oh," Jenna said, voice just above a whisper. She retreated back to her spot. The world continued to plod forward, exactly as it had done the moment after the car collision—the accident she'd caused.

Sucking in a breath when her wrist drug across an unseen thorn, Mercy soothed her hurt by eating another berry. Michael hummed along with his sister and Mercy avoided further thorns. She didn't want to end up looking like she'd been in a fight. At least blackberries couldn't cause black eyes.

When his bucket overflowed with berries, Michael backed out of his spot and Mercy followed suit. Jenna was already free of the patch, sitting against a tree and taking long draws from the canteen. Michael plopped onto the thin grass next to his sister. Again, Mercy found herself imitating her younger, wiser tutors and lowered herself to the ground.

"You filled that all by yourself?" Mercy couldn't fathom the elf-like girl had filled her own bucket before she and Michael had finished.

"Yup." One corner of Jenna's mouth turned up before she held up her purple-tipped fingers and wiggled them. "Small hands. I do this all the time. I know the secrets." Her dark eyes twinkled.

Michael stood. "Let's get back so we can get the cobbler in the solar oven before we lose all of the sun."

"Solar oven?" Mercy groaned as she hoisted her body up, muscles protesting. She took the full bucket from Michael, who had also grabbed the rake.

"You don't have solar ovens in the city?" Michael cocked his head sideways.

"I've never even heard of one."

"It's a box with a glass top. It works like a crockpot. Since the cobbler doesn't need much time, we can get home and bake it in a couple hours." Jenna switched her bucket from one hand to the other. "And our reg'lar oven scorches cobblers. It's nasty when it gets burnt."

Mercy couldn't imagine anything about blackberries being gross. "Let me carry both buckets," she offered. "You guys filled most of them, so I should carry."

Jenna smiled widely. "Okay."

Michael made noise the entire walk home, whistling and bouncing the rake. Then he began to sing off-key. "Go away snakes! Mercy doesn't like you. I don't like you either. But you're good to eat."

Mercy tripped and dumped some berries. "You eat rattlesnake?" She gagged.

"It tastes like chicken, but chewier." Michael pushed a long piece of hair behind his ears.

"Chicken?"

His eyes widened. "Please tell me you eat chicken in the city."

"We do. But rattlesnake tastes like chicken?"

Jenna's laughter bounced off of the trees. "It's kinda like chicken. We only have it once or twice a year, if Daddy or Uncle Robert kill one."

Mercy suppressed her retch.

"Have you eaten deer?"

"No."

"What about pheasant?"

"No."

"Turkey?" Michael stopped and turned, face scrunched as if she were an alien from another planet.

"I've had turkey!" Finally, something normal.

Jenna crinkled her pert nose. "Wild turkey or farm turkey?"

Mercy slowed her steps and lowered the buckets to the ground. "They're different?"

With an exasperated sigh, Michael grabbed one of the buckets and trudged away. Cowering in idiotic silence, Mercy trailed behind. Even farther behind, Jenna whistled a tune.

Still exhausted, Mercy blinked back the tears, feeling the weight of Michael's words. She had never been anywhere but the concrete jungle of New York City. Apartment buildings, dilapidated parks, and pot-holed streets had been her entire life until she stepped off the plane, then bus, into the small mountain farming town of Fayette, population 2,527 according to the bullet-pocked sign.

A tiny hand slipped into Mercy's and squeezed. "It's okay. We've never seen a skyscraper. I bet they are real tall."

"They are, kiddo. Real, real tall."

Chapter 2

"It's Sunday!" Adele kissed Mercy's forehead as the younger Benson woke. "Heather invited us to church this morning."

"Okay." Mercy had never gone to church. Ever. She kept her doubt to herself, wondering what fresh torture awaited her.

They each had a bowl of the tasteless cereal Adele preferred before dressing in their new home. The throw rugs barely kept the chill from their feet. "Heather said that it's very casual. They've been meeting in houses since the church burned down last year." Adele pulled her black knit cap low. "Some type of electrical fire."

The big house was quiet when they stepped out into the arctic blast of mountain morning air.

Adele heaved a shaky sigh. "I haven't been to a church service for a long time. I stopped going when Papa and I moved to the city."

Mercy had never seen the small, tattered orange Bible Adele clutched, as if someone would snatch it from her hands. She inched closer to Adele's elbow as the pair approached the house address Heather had written on a scrap of paper. The Kinnetts had left early to help set up so the Bensons walked down the side roads of Fayette.

More than a couple dozen men and women visited in groups on the front lawn, wrapped in jackets and sweaters to combat the frigid wind which pulled the colorful, dying leaves from the trees. Mercy jammed her hands farther into her old, brown jacket, wishing it had more warmth to offer. A slim, silver-haired woman welcomed Adele and Mercy, introducing herself as the homeowner, Julie. Mercy politely smiled and paid attention as other families arrived, their children romping on the small patch of brown grass. Remaining silent through the introductions, Mercy followed the older women into the house, offering a small, close-lipped smile to anyone who happened to make eye contact. She felt painfully ridiculous, just like each time she had to move schools and meet new teachers and kids.

"I think it's going to be a full house," Julie chuckled as they entered the large room in her sprawling home. "Pastor Ron has special news today." Her blue-as-the-sky eyes sparkled. Mercy thought it sounded like a good type of announcement, gauging by Julie's smile.

The entire room was twice as large as the guest house Mercy and Adele lived in, and already filled with people, elbow-to-elbow. Julie showed the newcomers to some folding chairs and Mercy opted to stand behind her mother-in-law in case someone else needed the seat.

Soon, a brunette sank into the chair next to Adele, after Mercy had motioned for the expectant mother to sit. She was about Mercy's age, and Mercy's heart tweaked in pain at the sight of her pregnant belly. Derrick had wanted kids. Mercy resisted the idea, certain she would make a horrible mother because of her own dysfunctional upbringing. Had Mercy bent to Derrick's pleas or promises that they would be different parents, she might have a piece of him—maybe a boy who had the same cowlick on the back of his head or a little girl with a crooked pinky. As it was, Mercy only had the cheap silver wedding ring that she spun round and round on her necklace while the expectant mother and Adele made small talk.

Tearing her eyes from the woman's belly, Mercy turned her interest to the room, scanning for anything, anyone to draw her attention away from the gnawing guilt in her brain. A few men were moving folding chairs closer together while mothers arranged their children on the wooden floors within reach. The press of bodies had warmed up the room. Mercy pulled her hands from the pockets of her jacket before unzipping the front.

"Can I hang that up for you?" Mercy swiveled to face the deep voice from behind her and was startled by the nearness of an unshaved face. His attractiveness and cologne caught her off guard.

"I…um…no. No, thank you." Mercy's words tumbled out all in one breath. She had fully anticipated an older man, like the ones moving the chairs and helping families settle in, not the face of a man a few years older than she, brown curls cropped near his neck and a couple of day's worth of stubble on his chin, scars criss-crossing his cheeks and nose. He smiled and his eyebrows arched up. His eyes. She tried to decide if they were blue or gray. Feeling a hot blush of embarrassment creep up her neck, Mercy turned forward again and rezipped her jacket. Just then, a gray-haired man raised his hands at the front of the room.

"Good morning!" he shouted, the joy obvious in his tone. As some folks answered back, the man spoke loudly again, "Let's try this again: good morning!" This time, a resounding response returned with the same words. Mercy tried not to flinch. "We are working with the County and it looks like our permit to rebuild the church is slated to be approved this week." Applause erupted throughout the room, and Mercy clapped because it seemed the right thing to do.

Across the crowd, Mercy caught sight of the man who had offered to take her jacket. He gathered coats, disappeared after obtaining an armful, and returned to start his task over again. His blue denim shirt had the sleeves rolled up to the elbows and everyone seemed to know him, surrendering their outerwear with ease. Mesmerized, Mercy watched as a young girl reached out toward him when he knelt next to the child's mother. He gathered the blond girl in one arm and coats in the other and vanished to the back of the crowd. Mercy silently chastised herself for being disappointed he was married.

She returned her attention to Pastor Ron when he opened a well-used book. Mercy guessed it was a Bible since he was a pastor and would probably be talking about the words inside. Around the room, people pulled out a menagerie of various Bibles onto their laps or cradled them close to their chests. Adele turned the pages of her tiny Bible just after Mercy caught the words "New Testament" on the cover. Her confusion blossomed. Was there an Old Testament in the Bible? The pages around the room fluttered, then grew quiet as Pastor Ron repeated where he would be reading from yet again: Ephesians. Mercy certainly couldn't spell the word, but she shifted on her feet and listened as Pastor Ron spoke.

He began with prayer. Mercy dropped her gaze to the floor when she saw the other adults in the room close their eyes. She didn't want to look as clueless as she felt. Pastor Ron thanked God for the opportunity for the congregation to meet, then switched to asking the Lord for protection for the people gathered together. A hushed round of "amens" circulated around the crowd. Mercy didn't have any idea what "amen" meant. She lifted her eyes, seeking the nearest exit, and was surprised to find the Jacket Man observing her far across the sea of people before returning his eyes to the sweet little girl he still carried, whispering into her ear.

"In Jesus' name, amen," Pastor Ron concluded. He breathed in and read from the book in his hands, pausing to read from a scrap of paper next to the text in his Bible. Mercy tried to grasp what Pastor Ron said, struggling to understand what the "will of God" and "spiritual blessings" were. She thought she might have it figured out a little until he continued, "Jesus chose us before the foundation of the world that we should be holy and blameless before Him."

Mercy's lungs tightened, and she moved a hand to grip the back of Adele's chair. Her knuckles turned white as she thought about the pastor's words. How in the world could she be blameless when she had been the reason Derrick tried to cross the street?

Throat swollen, Mercy blinked quickly to try and keep the onslaught of tears at bay. She didn't want to lose it in front of a room full of strangers. Her free hand curled into itself, the stubbed fingernails digging into her palm, barely keeping her thoughts focused.

All of the sudden, chairs were moving and Adele stood.

"You okay?" her mother-in-law asked. Mercy silently nodded her head, hoping Adele would take the most direct route to the doorway and then straight to the guest house. In her mind, she kept hearing Pastor Ron repeat, "Holy and blameless," in a taunting loop, knowing she had zero hope of reaching such a lofty status. Adele stopped to talk with Heather, so Mercy ducked and dodged her way to the front door. She completely forgot Jacket Man. Mercy stumbled outside to wait for Adele, who introduced herself to another new friend.

The little girl who'd snuggled into Jacket Man's arms earlier stood far from the crowd of other children her age kicking a ball back and forth. She stared off into the trees, her fingers twitching. A messy, blond braid snaked out from the adult-sized knitted hat nearly covering her eyes. In a sweet voice, the girl sang while her feet moved, one in front of the other, along the white line on the shoulder of the abandoned road. Then she arrived at a break in the paint. Almost startled from her trance, the golden-haired child shook her head, turned around and started back down the line, the way she had come, singing her song. As she grew closer, Mercy heard her words: "*Erre con erre, cigarro, erre con erre, barril. Rapido corren el carros, cargados de azucar al ferrocarril.*" Her small tongue rolled the Spanish words with precision.

Fascinated, Mercy silently moved near Julie's curb. The other kids ignored the focused girl, walking her line, reciting Spanish. Mercy's heart ached.

"Hello," Mercy said when the girl had come within a few feet of the curb. But the girl trudged on, eyes glued to the white line, fingers not twitching, but moving in time with the recitation.

"Hello?" Mercy repeated.

The girl reached the end of the line again and reversed directions.

"Zoey," her mother called out. A woman in her forties approached the girl, gently taking the child by the shoulders. "Zoey, it's time to go play with the ball."

"I do not like playing with the ball." The girl didn't whine. Instead, she sounded exasperated at the thought of any fun. Mercy had never heard a girl who appeared to be no older than five-years-old with such a seasoned tone of voice.

"I didn't ask your opinion, young lady. It is time to play with your ball to help your finger coordination." The woman dropped to her haunches, to the child's level. The girl's eyes never rose from the white line.

"I told you that I do not want to play with the ball, Mommy. I do not like the ball. My fingers do not like the ball. I will continue on this line for now." Mercy covered her mouth to hide her smile.

"Let's go, Zoey." Her mother stood, her hand firmly grasping the girl's.

With a hard yank away, the girl yelled, "I will not go play with the ball!" Mercy thought little Zoey would run, yet she remained rooted on the traffic line.

"Not an option at this point," countered her mother, recapturing the small hand and pulling Zoey from the beloved white line.

In a flurry of arms, legs and a high scream, the girl became a small tornado of fury. Her mother pulled Zoey to the grass near Mercy and wrapped her child into a tight hug. The woman trapped the girl's legs between her own. With expertise which could only have come with practice, the mother rocked and shushed her daughter while Zoey thrashed and wailed. Mercy was torn between the child's anguish and slipping away to not cause any further embarrassment to the pair.

Jenna appeared at Mercy's side. She approached the commotion and sat next to the duo. "Hey, Zoey. It'll be okay. Just take some deep breaths, okay? I can play ball with you if you want." She reached into the fray, which had calmed to Zoey's shaky breaths and her mother's murmurs, and latched onto her friend's hand. "I'll help you but you have to calm down first."

"Okay, Jenna," Zoey said through her mother's tight embrace.

No sooner had Zoey skipped off with Jenna than Adele appeared at Mercy's shoulder.

"I'm excited about having music next week," Adele said.

Mercy made a noise from the back of her throat.

"I haven't sung church music since I was a teenager."

"Hi." Both women turned to see Robert, his head bare of its baseball cap, hand extended.

"Good morning," Adele shook his hand.

Mercy mirrored her mother-in-law because it was polite. She was tired, confused by Pastor Ron's talk, and wanted to take a nap, despite the handsome man in front of her. Robert didn't look like Derrick, and his voice was too deep. Mercy didn't want to meet a guy. She wanted to cry. Or eat chocolate. Then, sleep.

"I didn't get a chance to meet you yesterday, 'cause I was late getting back to work. I'm Robert McIntyre, Heather's brother."

Adele tucked her hand into Mercy's elbow. "Nice to meet you, Robert. I'm Adele, this is my … this is Mercy." The younger woman didn't miss the edited title: daughter-in-law. Adele meant well, but this was too obvious.

Robert dipped his head in Mercy's direction. "Nice to meet you, too. Heather tells me you're from New York City."

When Mercy remained silent, Adele eventually spoke. "We are. I moved there when I was younger, but Mercy lived there her whole life."

"Big change."

"It is," Adele said, stifling a yawn. "I think we are going to head back to the house now. The time change really has us turned around."

Eyes to the ground, Mercy watched Robert's worn shoes move away. Adele tugged Mercy back toward the guest house.

Mercy dropped into her own thoughts, shifting from Zoey, to Robert, and finally plunged into regret for her past. Though she had sworn off alcohol, her body ached for the way it drowned memories—the release from reality. She longed to forget she was a widow, poor and living in a guest house by the generosity of her mother-in-law and a distant relative. If Derrick were alive, they'd drink to the past or the future and laugh in the face of uncertainty. But he was buried on the other side of the country, and she endured with only memories.

Adele stayed noiseless long after they arrived at their new home, crawling straight into bed. Guilt clawed Mercy's soul about that, too. Adele had lost her husband to a freak incident with wasps, her oldest son to a workplace accident, and her youngest child to a car collision, all within twelve months of one another. Yet she remained optimistic despite it all.

As quietly as possible, Mercy filled their cleaning bucket with water and a splash of bleach and worked on disinfecting the bathroom and kitchen counters to keep her body moving. If she stopped, her mind would wander back to the dark places of her past and Pastor Ron's claims about holiness.

Near midafternoon, Adele woke and Mercy took a break from her chores. Adele made a huge fuss, delighted to see the freshly scrubbed floors, and that the dusty curtains had been washed and were rehung to drip dry. Mercy put together an early dinner of lunch meat, cheese, and the last of a loaf of bread Adele had baked the day before while Mercy and the twins were blackberry picking.

"I forgot to tell you," Adele said, swallowing the last of her cheese with a gulp of water. "Heather gave me a box of warm clothes from the attic. Maybe we can find something useful before the snow starts."

Found clothes? Mercy wondered if Heather's story was true or if she only wanted the women in her guest house feel less awkward over hand-me-down clothes. Neither Adele nor Heather had any idea that most of Mercy's new clothing throughout her life came by way of her own sticky fingers and unsuspecting store clerks.

"How did you like the sermon?"

Adele's question made Mercy's hand stop in the air before she set her plate onto the counter. "Holy and blameless" bounced between her ears. She looked at the dirty dishes before she answered. "It was fine."

"Did you understand it?" Adele brought her plate to Mercy at the sink.

"Not really. I never read the Bible." Mercy kept her tone even and regulated. She wanted to move on from the topic. Maybe next week she would understand more, but right now she wanted to forget the holy and blameless part—the role she could never hope to achieve.

"I'll see if there is an extra Bible for you."

The box Heather had left for the pair yielded freshly laundered, yet faded sweaters in a variety of colors. The old radio they had brought with them from the apartment cranked out wordless piano tunes while sweaters were inspected.

It had been dark for a few hours when the Benson women tucked their new clothes into the closet and readied themselves for bed. Mercy unfolded the stubborn couch out from itself before checking the door and two windows to make sure they were latched.

Mercy switched off the lone lamp and hunkered down to the comfortable side of the sofa bed. She had learned the hard way that the other side had two broken springs. The bleach-tainted air from the thin curtains magnified Mercy's satisfaction with the amount of work she had accomplished.

But she had to stay busy to keep Derrick's void and the unattainable holiness at bay. Just before she drifted off, she reminded herself to ask Heather about finding work. Studying birds and picking blackberries wouldn't cut it.

Chapter 3

Something roused Mercy from her sleep. She couldn't decide if it had been a dream, a nightmare, or just the annoying bird which kept changing its tune outside of their home. Jenna had said it was a mockingbird when Mercy had first been enchanted by its multiple songs. They were not as charming in the breaking dawn. Her waning enthusiasm about the gray bird's call made her growl in her throat before tossing the blanket aside.

She pulled on her boots and gathered the blankets onto the back of the couch before folding the bed back inside and replacing the cushions. Her mother-in-law stirred in her bed several feet away, under Jenna's pink and frilly castoff comforter. Adele had clearly been enchanted by it. "I've never had anything like it! I had Henry and the boys, so nothing was ever pink."

Mercy crept to the tiny bathroom and dressed in the nicest clothes she owned, a brown pair of pants and an old blue sweater of Derrick's. The sweater draped loosely on her frame, but Mercy tucked the bottom into her jeans and tugged at the neckline until it resembled something less masculine. It would have to suffice in case she was interviewed while searching for jobs. As a bonus, the sweater covered most of her tattoos. She didn't need extra judgement for the artwork. Brushing her hair out and over her ears to combat the chilly air, Mercy then pinched some color into her cheeks before brushing her teeth.

She pulled on her coat and stopped in the open room. Her nose started to run from the chill. Mercy fetched her blankets and piled them on top of Adele, then kissed her mother-in-law's cold cheek. "I'm going up to the house to talk with Heather about getting a job," Mercy whispered. She hated to leave before she made Adele breakfast, but the need to earn money to buy food and support her little family far outweighed anything else.

The air outside made Mercy wrap her arms around her middle. She hustled to the back door of the Kinnett's home. Seeing the kitchen light on, she knocked softly, hoping Robert wasn't there. It was too cold to wait until her awkwardness around a guy passed. Heather pulled open the door and invited Mercy into the empty room.

"I think it's going to freeze soon," Heather whispered, turning off the burner under her tea kettle. She pulled down a second mug without asking. Heather pulled the tea bag from the first cup and left it to steep in the second cup. She handed the first cup to Mercy and asked, "Are you okay?"

Mercy gratefully wrapped her fingers around the mug, nodding. "Yeah. I just…I need…" Her embarrassment warmed her body under the layers of clothing. "I want to know where I can get a job."

"I'm glad you asked, actually." Heather motioned for Mercy to sit with her. "I had a friend ask me about finding someone to clean his business for him. Would that work?"

Mercy's nervousness evaporated and left hopefulness in its wake. "That'd be perfect," she murmured, before blowing on her tea. "I did janitorial work back home."

"Great! I'll write down the address and directions for you. It's at a restaurant he owns." Heather scratched down information on the back of a used envelope. "I've known him all of my life. He's only two years younger than me but we went to school together until I graduated. I headed to medical school and he went into the service."

Mercy mentally calculated his age: thirty-six. She took the envelope Heather offered and listened as Heather outlined the directions to get to the restaurant.

"It's about a twenty-minute walk from here." The Kinnetts owned two trucks, but Mercy would never presume to ask to borrow one from Heather, since she made house calls, as Adele had explained during the bus ride. Heather's husband David, would be home from his night shift soon with the other truck.

"Until it starts snowing, then you'll have to get a head start," Heather added with a wink over her own tea.

Mercy thanked Heather for the tea and left, directions tucked into her jacket pocket. The sun rose but remained muted behind an expansive cloud cover. The chilling temperature hastened Mercy's steps toward her goal. As she walked, the houses and businesses of Fayette remained relatively untouched from the times they were built: picket fences and steep roof lines. It was nothing like the cement high rises which shaped New York. This town persisted in the cliché "no one locks their doors" era.

The neighborhood homes crowded closer as Mercy approached the main road. Though she had been in Fayette for just over two days, she hadn't glimpsed the heartbeat of the community. Stores and businesses were stacked side by side, like a scene from an old western film she had seen in school. She half expected a horse to be tied outside of the row of buildings, one of them christened "Saloon."

"On your left!" called out a man's voice from behind. A bicycle breezed by her tucked-in left elbow, dodging a hole in the pocked asphalt. Mercy strained to see the bicyclist's headlamp pull into a parking lot jammed with trucks, in front of a large barn at the end of the main street. Squinting, she could just make out the sign above the massive doors: The Broken Big Horn—her destination.

The ancient and massive wooden barn bookended the far side of Fayette's main thoroughfare. Although the big doors were shut tight, customers entered through a smaller door to the right. The closer Mercy walked, the stronger the smell of bacon and the louder the conversations that bled out each time the door opened. Her heart picked up its pace when she stepped forward and pulled the door handle. She had to get this job, no matter the pay or hours, whether scrubbing toilets or washing dishes.

Her stomach appreciated the smell of warm food. Mercy walked inside the rustic barn, surprised by the wooden floors. She had fully expected hard-packed dirt or straw under the dozen or so diners. An apple-shaped woman, hair pulled up under a well-worn cowboy hat and wearing a half apron, approached Mercy, who remained rooted just inside of the door.

"Hey there!" The waitress' generous smile matched the mirth in her brown eyes. "Table for one?" Her hand-written name tag declared she was Kimberly.

Mercy shifted on her feet. "Um, no. I…ah…Heather, I mean Dr. Kinnett, told me the owner needed some extra help cleaning."

"Sure! Wyatt had said you might be coming in and to introduce you to Hank." Kimberly put her hand on Mercy's elbow and led her through the mismatched tables. "Hank's our cook. He'll get ya started but you'll mostly be working in the afternoon and at night, after we shut down." The cowboy-hat clad waitress called out a hello to someone by name who had just entered, then steered Mercy through the swinging double doors leading to the kitchen.

Hank topped out near six feet, seven inches, with no spare meat on his frame. He wielded a metal spatula and wore a striped apron. Standing next to

Kimberly, Mercy's mind instantly leapt to the childhood saying: Jack Sprat could eat no fat, his wife could eat no lean! She hid a smile as he greeted them over the large stove.

"This is the young gal Wyatt told us about." Kimberly grabbed an order Hank had just put onto a plate. "What's your name, hon?"

"It's, ah, Mercy." She had pressed herself tight against the wall near the doors and still felt like she stood in the way. Mercy resisted the desire to unzip her jacket though the warmth from the stove had driven away the chill.

"Nice to meet ya, Mercy," Kimberly said. She nodded then pushed back through the doors with her orders.

"Have you had breakfast yet?" Hank nudged some cut up potatoes in a skillet the size of three dinner plates.

Though her empty stomach begged her to say she hadn't, Mercy's self-respect answered that she wasn't hungry. It would go against every instinct she had to accept free food when she was trying to get a job there. She listened as Hank laid out the business while processing orders Kimberly dropped and retrieved. As the sole cook, he and Kimberly, the waitress, occasionally had help from someone named Felicity. The "Big Horn family" generally got along and believed another hand to help with the workload would be perfect.

"You'll be our go-to girl." Hank laughed, flipping a pancake on the griddle. "You'll be here to let Kimmy and me get home at a decent hour." He paused his work and his bushy white eyebrows furrowed together. "Will you be okay with getting home on your own in the dark?"

"Yup," Mercy said, even though the thought of walking home in the middle of the night with a flashlight was unappealing. She'd find a nice, solid stick to thwart any rattlesnakes. "I'll be fine."

Hank continued to outline the ebb and flow of the restaurant. Most customers were from the surrounding community. An expansive garden and greenhouse occupied the area behind the barn because they'd "gone organic" a few years back. Hank tilted his head toward a door and told Mercy to "take a gander."

The sturdy metal door stuck, and Mercy yanked on the handle until it opened. She shivered in the shade under the small overhang, and the garden directly off the cement slab had more brown than green leaves. To the right, a greenhouse had been built into the sloping hill, its windows a menagerie of mismatched panes gathering the rising sun. Great rows of pumpkins lined shelves under its eaves. A few orange rejects remained in the brown field where some errant chickens happily pecked at them.

Mercy stepped into the greenhouse. Moist warmth permeated the air that smelled like onions and wet earth. She had never seen a greenhouse in person and crouched to study the neat, green rows planted in the ground. The glass ceiling sloped, well over seven feet up on the high side, dropped to four feet across the large room. The tall side's wall was composed of tires stacked flat on top of each other from dirt floor to the windowed ceiling.

Having no idea as to which plants were which, Mercy craned her neck both ways, to get a general sense of the layout before she retreated back into the kitchen. Hank pushed a plate laden with potatoes and eggs toward her. Mercy angled her body into a corner and ate in silence, despite her earlier refusal. Kimberly and Hank worked in a well-oiled tandem, processing orders.

Dirty dishes had started accumulating near the sink by the time Mercy finished her breakfast. She shed her jacket and pushed up the sleeves of her sweater. Hank nodded the location of the soap and she got to work, elbow deep in suds on one side of the sink. The cook told Mercy to fill the bucket in the sink with clean water to rinse. "We'll use it to water the greenhouse," he explained. "Organic-y kind of thing."

Happy to be busy versus awkwardly watching the duo work, Mercy made her way through the stack of dishes. Twice, she emptied the rinse bucket into a large funnel in the wall which Hank said fed the underground watering system.

"Child, what a blessing you've been this morning!" Kimberly delivered the last of the dishes a couple of hours later. When the older woman gave her a one-armed shoulder embrace, Mercy froze with her hands in the rinse bucket. She had always been wary of hugs, with the exceptions of Adele and Derrick, as they usually preceded some type of request, from her experience. "Now, I'll have time to show you around before I go." Kimberly unceremoniously dumped a plate full of silverware into the soapy sink.

The restaurant was almost empty, with the exception of a table occupied by a young woman who cut her meal into tiny pieces to share with the small girl at the table with her. Kimberly gave a thorough tour, explaining how the big barn doors were bolted shut to create a shelter and how the old hay loft had been converted to use as a sleeping area for anyone in an emergency.

"Like … what kind of emergency?" Mercy looked up to the second floor and imagined bodies lying next to one another, like the flop houses she and Derrick would crash in for a night or two when they were too drunk to come home.

"Anything Wyatt deems is a crisis. Could be their house burned down. Or we've had a family of travelers stay up there once."

Mercy made a noise that she hoped sounded thoughtful or agreeable.

Kimberly's laughter rang loud and bounced off the barn rafters. "You haven't met Wyatt, have you?"

"No." Suddenly, Mercy thought she might be missing the punchline of a joke. Maybe she *was* the punchline to the joke.

"Honey, Wyatt Peralta is the owner. He's not much older than you, but he has a heart for the lost since his mama died last year."

Mercy refused to ask questions about Wyatt. She'd known the pressure to be under scrutiny when someone close died. Even mundane questions could trigger tears. She tugged down her sleeves to cover the tattoos.

As if she could sense Mercy's emotions shift, Kimberly pulled Mercy farther into the Big Horn.

"Here's the office. Wyatt does all the paperwork and stuff back here. I don't have a head for numbers, but he seems to do alright." She inclined her head to a door with a curtained window. "Wyatt keeps the door locked. We may help folks out, but they've helped themselves out a time or two, so he's the only one who goes in there."

The circuit ended where it had begun, at the kitchen. As they pushed through the doors, tears sprung to Mercy's eyes. Hank sat on the chair Mercy had vacated in the corner, peeling an onion. The smell punched Mercy's sinuses and she coughed into the crook of her elbow.

"You'll get used to it." The cook grinned and continued his duty.

With his words, Mercy turned to Kimberly, jaw slack in disbelief. "I got the job?"

"Of course you did, hon."

"Can I run home and let my mother-in-law know? It'll only take a half hour at the most—I'll jog." Mercy's excitement caused the sentence to mash together like a colossal run-on word.

Kimberly laughed and scooted Mercy out of the door. She sped by mailboxes and dogs barking behind their fences. She'd never seen so many dismantled cars than in the yard next to the Kinnett's beautiful home.

Adele sat on the couch, sipping a cup of tea when Mercy rushed in through the door.

"I got it!"

Without regard to her modesty, Mercy tore off her sweater and shucked her pants, throwing on her dirty, worn jeans and a hoodie. Adele laughed as Mercy hopped and pulled at the clothing while explaining her 'interview.'

Mercy retied her shoes and her fingers stilled.

"I don't even know what days or time I work."

Adele's soft hand patted her shoulder.

"Does it matter?" Adele knew the desperation of poverty and hunger as well as Mercy did after they both were widowed and lost their jobs.

"No. It doesn't."

Chapter 4

Breathless from running, Mercy arrived back to the Big Horn with three minutes to spare. The air hung thick from toxic onion slices in preparation for dinner. Hank explained the restaurant had a set menu that was written on the calendar near the front door, and it would be pulled pork with grilled onions and fried squash this particular evening. He handed Mercy a knife and they chopped the yellow and white squashes into small squares. Hank gave her nothing but encouragement when she worried over the lack of uniformity in her pieces.

"Do you know anything about the squash we're working with?"

"Not a thing," Mercy admitted, trying to keep her focus on the white one that resembled a flower.

Hank enlightened his student on the types of vegetables they cut and put them into lightly salted water. "It helps keep the squash fresh before we cook it."

Mercy's fingers were pruned by the time they had filled three huge buckets. "Where did Kimberly go?"

"She goes home in the middle of the day. We don't serve lunch."

Busy in the kitchen, Mercy hadn't noticed the lack of patrons.

"Do you go home?" she asked.

"Sometimes. Most times, I stay here and get ready for dinner. I'm glad Wyatt brought you aboard cause then I can go home after dinner and get some sleep." Up close, Mercy could see the weariness manifested in dark half circles under his eyes. "I'm getting too old to be burning the candle at both ends."

Hank showed Mercy the pantry, explaining the way the rows were arranged. She had to remember to keep her mouth shut. So much food.

"Why are some of them in glass jars?"

"You've never seen canned veggies before?" The disbelief in Hank's voice triggered Mercy's defensive mode.

"I grew up in the city."

"No need to get jumpy, missy. I've lived out here my whole life and I'm sure if we were in the city, you could teach me a few things."

Mercy's hackles soothed down at his calm, slow drawl. "I'm sorry. I feel upside down without sidewalks and tall buildings." She pulled her finger across the rows of beans, still amazed at the copious amount of food.

Hank led her back to the greenhouse and rattled off the names of the rows of plants. In the dying garden outside, he showed her how to check for hidden vegetables. Mercy suppressed a squeal when she found a yellow crookneck squash tucked under some scratchy leaves. The pair continued down the rows, Mercy learning how to tell if an onion or garlic was ready for harvest and how long they stayed in cold storage. She knew she couldn't remember it all in a day, but tried to mentally file what she could. Then they went back inside and Hank made a couple of quesadillas.

"In that closet over there," Hank said, pointing to a door next to the bathroom off of the kitchen, "you'll find the tools and stuff. Kimmy and I can't be climbing the ladder and there's a few lightbulbs that need to be replaced. Think you can do that while I start dinner?"

Mercy shouldered the ladder out to the dining area, bulbs tucked into her hoodie pocket. She switched out six lights, humming along to the radio perched near the cash register. It cranked out the same classic rock that Papa Benson loved to sing. When she returned to the kitchen to ask Hank about sweeping, she found him propped against a wall, mouth relaxed and open. Snoring.

Broom in hand, Mercy returned back to the dining room and swept all of the food and trash into a corner until she could find a dustpan. Dinner wouldn't start for another two hours, according to the plastic soda pop clock. The front door hadn't moved at all, so she stole back into the supply closet for a duster to tackle the build-up on the light fixtures.

Somewhere between shoving the ladder from one table to the next, Mercy moved to the music, hips swaying to the beat. She flicked the duster to the ceiling, using the handle as her lip sync microphone. She was well into the second verse of the song when she spotted someone leaning against the wall near the office.

Jacket Man.

With a grin as wide as the Hudson River.

"Please," he said, uncrossing his arms and twirling one hand in front of himself, "don't let me interrupt."

The duster dropped to Mercy's side. She stared at the floor, paralyzed between mortification and bolting for the door.

His chuckle spiked her feet to the floor. "Aw, I'm sorry I scared you. Don't mean to frighten the new help."

Mercy studied her shoes. Her free hand dug into her jeans as he moved.

The well-worn work boots stopped closer than she'd like, but far enough away to make her hold her breath. A calloused hand extended into sight.

"I'm Wyatt, your boss."

Out of sheer manners, Mercy shook his hand, trying to touch the least amount of skin. "Mercy Benson." She pulled her hand back to her side and jammed it into her pocket.

"You're Cousin Adele's daughter."

"Daughter-in-law," she mumbled.

Wyatt laughed again. "My bad. Apologies." His boots backed up and disappeared from Mercy's view. "Is Hank here?"

"He's in the kitchen. I'll go get him." Mercy turned before Wyatt could answer. She practically sprinted to the kitchen, hitting the wooden door harder than she intended and jolted Hank from his nap. "Wyatt is here."

Hank groaned as he stood. The door pushed open behind Mercy. Hank lifted his chin. "Hey, Boss."

"What's for dinner?" Wyatt stepped around Mercy and toward the stove, sniffing the air.

The men began talking about food, allowing Mercy to escape to the dining hall. As the door swung shut, she heard Wyatt's question, "She's a flighty little thing, isn't she?"

With cautious glimpses toward the kitchen door, Mercy sped through the last of the dusting. She was prepared when Wyatt approached this time.

"Sorry I can't offer you anything but a part-time position," he said. "But it's sure a big help to Kimberly and Hank."

Mercy forced her shoulders straight. "Thank you for the job. I really appreciate it."

"Feel free to help yourself to whatever meal you want while you're here. And take any leftovers home. They just go into the trash, otherwise."

"Thank you," she said, hoping the flat tone would mask her surprise. She'd climbed into dumpsters for food before, out of desperation. "Freeganism" another person had told her, uncovering an entire takeout box of stir fry chicken in triumph. Mercy had felt nothing but humiliation.

"You're not much of a talker, are you?"

Mercy didn't answer. She peeked at the kitchen door over his shoulder, hoping Hank would come in and save her from a conversation with this stranger— her boss.

"Did Kimberly happen to tell you about the party next Saturday?"

"No." Her single syllable dragged out a few seconds.

"Man, you got an accent! What part of New York are you from?"

She edited her answer before responding because he probably didn't know the city anyways. "Queens." And it wasn't a lie. That's where the Bensons lived and took her into their apartment. Third story walk-up with leaky plumbing.

"Murray Hill? Jamaica?"

Mercy's cheek twitched as he rattled off the suburbs. A sharp knock at the front door before it pulled open spared her response.

"Hello?" called a feminine voice straight from a fairytale movie.

Wyatt turned, his eyebrows lifted. "Hey, Felicity."

"I hoped I'd catch you here." Once the door closed and her eyes adjusted, Mercy could see that Felicity's beauty matched her voice: wavy, blond hair flowing down her back, a toothpaste ad smile, and prettiness without even a trace of makeup on her face. All of this combined with her fleece-lined leather jacket, heeled boots, and perfectly fitted jeans made

Mercy want to melt into a puddle of ugly on the floor. It was like having every Disney princess wrapped into one impossibly lovely woman.

"Oh hi," Felicity said, peeking around Wyatt. "You must be Mercy." She offered her hand.

Mercy shook it quickly and retracted. "Hi."

Wyatt nodded between them. "Felicity Bailey, Mercy Benson. She's working here now."

"Oh, that's fantastic!" Felicity smiled perfect rows of bleached teeth, a dimple burrowing into both cheeks. "Kimberly told me last week how exhausted she's been. He's a slave driver, this one." Her adoring gaze turned to the bearded man at her side.

For a moment, Mercy focused on the pair: Wyatt's scars etched deep into his skin, disappearing beneath his dark, shaggy beard in sharp contrast to the blush on Felicity's face. The way they watched each other made her ache for Derrick, and how he rubbed his thumb in circles in the small of her back or traced the feathers on her elbow.

Wyatt nodded his head toward Mercy. "I was going to tell her about the party."

"Oh my goodness," Felicity said, clapping her hands together. "I'm so excited for it this year! I have all of the decorations ready and Kimberly will be so grateful for the extra set of hands."

"I'm glad I can help," Mercy said, feeling as useful as a screen door on a submarine for the moment.

Felicity reached over and squeezed Mercy's bicep. "I gotta get back to work, but I'm sure we'll talk again. I'll text you later," she added, moving her hand to Wyatt's forearm. And in a whirlwind of floral perfume and song, Felicity hummed her way back out of the front door.

"I need to get going, too," Wyatt said. He scratched the scar crossing the bridge of his nose. "Never a dull moment here."

Mercy retreated back to the kitchen. Hank rummaged in the pantry while Mercy washed her hands in the sink. She used the stubby brush next to the faucet to get under her nails, cringing from the scalding water.

"Give that pot a stir," Hank called out.

"Which one?" She wasn't sure if she should stir the onions or the mystery in the covered pot that spread across two burners.

"The one with the cover."

When Mercy moved the lid, steam smacked her face, then the smell of barbeque. Using the wooden paddle on the counter and both hands, Mercy shoved the meat around in a circle. Hank appeared at her elbow. "Like this?" She panted, switching directions.

"That's perfect. Just a couple more times and then put the lid back on."

"It smells delicious."

"Family recipe, right there. Cooked it overnight."

"How do you do that?"

"In an oven."

Mercy set the paddle down and moved the lid back. She had no idea how a restaurant wouldn't burn down if the oven was left on.

"Low and slow," Hank said. "You leave the oven on as low as it will go and just cook it for hours."

"Like a crockpot?"

"Eh." He swiped his thumb across the paddle, tasting the pork. "It's good. But, see here." Hank pushed a piece of paper toward Mercy. "I need you to go give this to Wyatt for his supply run down the hill tomorrow."

"Okay." She had no idea what any of that meant, but she'd do it. "Where is he?"

"Probably back in his office. Likes to do the bookkeeping between shifts or late at night, when he's not in the fields."

No way she would ask Hank what he meant by that. Maybe Wyatt stood in a field before work each day.

"He runs alfalfa fields."

Her eyebrows bucked down before she could stop them. "Alfalfa?" She shook her head.

"It's a type of feed that they grow in the fields for horses and cattle. Wyatt is trying to get the second crop baled before the rains start."

"He had a first crop?"

Hank smiled, his uneven yellowing teeth in sharp contrast to the whites of his eyes. "You and me are going to have to have a country talk sometime. You write down any questions you have and I'll answer them straight up."

"Rattlesnakes," she said. An involuntary shiver slithered down her spine. "The kids told me they live around here."

"They do. Most likely you won't see any. Just remember this … you listening?" He pointed his finger and waited for Mercy to nod. "Triangle head and you're dead."

"Okay."

Hank inhaled and a chuckle pushed through his long nose. "Better yet, you just stay away from any snakes, missy. Now go on and give this to the boss."

Mercy went to the dining area and back to the place Kimberly had pointed out earlier. She knocked on the frame of the open office door. "Hank wanted me to give you the supply list for tomorrow." There was a dark leather couch to her right with an ugly purple blanket draped over the arm and a colossal desk to the left, covered in various stacks of papers and pens.

Wyatt's back faced her, arm muscles taut as he brought down a paint brush, covering the white wall with a stripe of blue. He looked back over his shoulder, jaw working a piece of gum. "Huh?"

She stepped into the office and repeated Hank's request. Wyatt turned, brush suspended mid-air. A bright glob of pink rested deep in his beard.

"Uh. You have something stuck there … in your beard." Mercy bobbed her head toward his face, hoping he'd catch on.

"What?" Wyatt reached up and stopped short. "Oh gross. I just ate a piece of taffy before I started." He stared at his paint-splashed hands and dripping brush. "Would you mind helping me out? There's some napkins right there." He nodded to the edge of his desk.

Mercy hesitated and then grabbed a handful of paper napkins. Wyatt held one hand under his paint brush, catching the drips in his palm. She tried to tug the pink goo free, but it worked farther into his curly hair.

"Oh come on," she whispered, leaning in.

"I'm glad I'm not the only one who talks or dances with inanimate objects."

Mercy jerked her shoulders back and glimpsed up to his eyes, fingers tangled in his beard. She hadn't touched a man's face since the night Derrick died.

Wyatt smiled and then wiggled the paint brush again. "Sorry. I'll let you finish."

After a bit of prodding and picking, the last of the taffy pulled free. Her hands had started to shake. Mercy wasn't sure if it was because of her nerves or because their bodies nearly touched one another. She wadded up the napkins and tossed them into the trashcan in the corner.

"Thank you."

"Sure." She opened her mouth to speak and then clamped it closed again.

"What?"

"You should trim that so it doesn't get food stuck in it."

"Maybe."

Wyatt moved back to the half stroke on the wall. He wiped his wet palm onto his jeans. "Mom only let me paint my room once because I used to make such a mess," he said, pondering the slash of blue on his pants. "You like painting?"

"I've never done it before."

"Well, go grab a brush from the closet."

Mercy scrambled for an answer. She didn't want to be stuck in the room with a handsome stranger, who

48

happened to be her boss. "I think I should check with Hank to see if I need to do anything before dinner." She backed toward the door.

Wyatt clicked his tongue. "Good idea, since that is what you're here for."

She turned and was almost to the kitchen when Kimberly entered the front door. "Honey, you look like you're running from a ghost."

Mercy couldn't disagree, still haunted by Wyatt's cologne—the same kind Derrick used to wear.

Chapter 5

Standing beneath the canopy, Mercy twisted to see hundreds of thin strips of torn fabric, frayed ropes, and ribbons strung up between an enormous steel frame behind the Big Horn, courtesy of Felicity's work over the last week and a half. Line after line of miniature white Christmas lights were strung high overhead. There were haphazard areas of folding chairs and old pieces of carpet on the grass nearby. An assortment of solar lights had been pushed into the ground. Mercy had never seen anything so comical and romantic in her life. She could already imagine the dancing once everyone arrived, grateful she would be away from the action. Well-intentioned strangers would ask her questions and she wanted to stay invisible.

She hurried across the concrete dance floor, under the ribbons and soft lights, as if its magic would taint her memories with Derrick. Mercy wasn't ready to move on from him. Especially in a town full of unfamiliar people. Kimberly waved her over to the outdoor serving area, a handful of tables end to end, laden with covered dishes.

"Why aren't you all dressed up, missy?" Kimberly clucked her tongue while rolling plastic cutlery into napkins.

Mercy felt her cheeks flush crimson. She had dressed up as best as her wardrobe allowed, in a blue button up shirt and some khaki pants she promised to reserve for church on Sundays. Mercy didn't respond. Instead, she turned her attention to rolling a knife, spoon and fork into each napkin before depositing the tableware into a basket. Poverty proved bitter, including the lack of appropriate clothing.

Kimberly mumbled about "fetching something from the Big Horn" and disappeared. Mercy was left alone to her task, content to simply work without having to talk to anyone or make excuses for her wardrobe.

As she neared the end of her task, several men arrived, toting various instruments: guitars, drums, and even a piano on a wheeled platform. Hank pushed the piano from behind while Wyatt pulled and walked backwards. Felicity appeared and trotted toward the group, her fingers playing a tune while she walked, as the men worked the black piano into place near the canopy. Released from his towing duty, Wyatt turned and tipped the front of his cowboy hat at Mercy with a smile.

When Mercy dropped her eyes, they fell to her blue shirt. Felicity had a pink, patterned dress with a skirt that fell to her calves and soft curls around her shoulders. Mercy threw the last of the silverware into the basket, then jerked her hand back when she saw Wyatt standing on the opposite of the table, looking at her.

"I gotta go get my apron," she blurted, turning on her heels and fleeing.

The lump in her throat grew so big by the time Mercy reached the safety of the Big Horn's back door that she thought she might choke. With no other clothes to change into, she went to the bathroom to see if anything could be done with her hair to resemble "dressed up."

Once in front of the mirror with the door locked, Mercy let down her hair from its ever-present bun and ran her fingers through it to pull apart the brown, wavy curls. First she parted her hair to the left, then the right. Both styles neither satisfied her nor passed for natural. Sweeping the hair from both sides of her face and securing it with her hair tie, Mercy arranged the loose strands from the back of her head behind her shoulders. She pinched her skin up and down the cheekbone and color flooded under her freckles.

Wetting her lips, Mercy glared at her reflection and wondered what in the world she was doing. She had no one to impress. Felicity's bubbly personality, flawless curls, and pink dress amazed more than just the men. And while Mercy's thoughts pulled toward Wyatt, he deserved someone who complimented him in every way which Mercy could not. Her hands went to yank out the half ponytail when a knock at the bathroom door caused her to jump.

"Mercy?" Kimberly called from the other side of the door.

Mercy pulled the doorknob instead of the ponytail. "Sorry I took so long. I just … didn't have time to do my hair at home because I thought I'd be late." She flicked off the light switch and maneuvered to pass her coworker.

"You look real pretty," Kimberly said, smiling. "I remembered that I forgot to give you this the other day," she continued, thrusting a bunch of light green material at Mercy. "It used to be mine. I had thought I'd give it to my daughter one day, but then the good Lord blessed me with my boys instead!"

Mercy had no idea what the green fabric was, or what to say. She held up part of the material and straightened it out until it hung from her hands. "It's a dress?"

"Well, yes it is! You've seen them before, I take it." Kimberly chuckled. "I think you may be skinnier than I used to be, but there is a tie at the waist so you can cinch it up real nice." The older woman inspected the dress held in the air between the two of them, her relaxed smile full of reminiscence.

"I couldn't possibly take your dress." Mercy pushed the pale cotton dress dotted with miniature flowers back toward its owner. "You should save it and give it to one of your boys' wives when they are older."

Kimberly took two steps backwards and held up both of her hands. "Don't tell me who I should give my dress to, Mercy Benson. It's mine and I'm giving it to you." She folded her arms. "I'd be highly offended if you didn't wear it tonight."

Overwhelmed by Kimberly's generosity, Mercy murmured, "okay," in order to keep from crying.

"Good! I'll go put these spoons out on the table and be back in to make sure it doesn't need pinning or nothing." Kimberly left with a smile.

Mercy turned on the bathroom light once more and changed into the dress. Cut in a modest "V" at the neckline, the bottom hem brushed her feet. Half sleeves hid most of her tattoos, leaving her favorite rose and mandala exposed on her forearm. After pulling the ribbons at the waist and tying them behind her, Mercy twirled in the tiny bathroom. She wouldn't admit to anyone that she had never owned a dress. The pale green material made her freckles less noticeable, she thought after another turn in the mirror. Removing her tennis shoes, Mercy knew she would be much colder later in the evening. It made her a bit giddy knowing she would sacrifice comfort for beauty. Her only regret was the lack of fresh, pretty polish for her toenails.

She folded her pants and shirt, then tucked them with her shoes into the cupboard under the sink so she could change before she returned home later.

She heard the back door squeak open and knew Kimberly had returned. Pulling in a deep breath to steady her nerves, Mercy turned the light off. She backed out of the bathroom and closed the door, taking a few more seconds to build up the courage to thank Kimberly. With no other choice than to turn around, Mercy spun on her heels and sucked in her breath when she saw Wyatt.

"I thought you were Kimberly." Her cheeks were on fire again.

"No. I came to check on you. You'd been gone awhile and I thought your apron might've grown legs and walked off." He'd removed his cowboy hat and held it to his chest, as if he would launch into the pledge of allegiance. He grinned. "And that is a nice apron."

"Thank you," Mercy said, desperate to find her apron which, of course, hung behind Wyatt near the door. She sidestepped the man and fished her apron from the hook.

"Need any help?"

The kitchen was suddenly too small.

"No."

She hurried back to the outdoor table while tying her own apron strings.

The sun began its descent and solar lights joined the overhead lights to illuminate the area. Packs of townspeople arrived: families, teenagers, even toddlers on their tricycles. Even Adele appeared on Robert's arm with Heather and her family. Mercy moved behind the serving table and caught Kimberly's hand. She squeezed Kimberly's fingers in gratitude, knowing she might not be able to speak without melting into a thankful, blubbering mess. The older woman returned Mercy's smile and then seamlessly directed the younger worker to start uncovering the food.

Across the ribboned canopy, the piano sounded just before Felicity's voice. As if the song triggered some unseen force, the Big Horn's table was trounced by hungry folks. Michael made two trips through the line. Mercy and Kimberly worked in tandem, refilling chicken and sautéed potatoes, or helping mothers carry their children's plates to the grass.

Between refilling the food and shuttling dirty pans to the Big Horn's kitchen to wash later, Mercy reveled in the sights. Children ran around the solar lights, playing tag or dancing without a care for the rhythm. Soon, adults filtered onto the dance area, laughing and spinning their way through fast songs or enjoying the closeness of a slower tempo. Some men danced with their little girls on their shoes. Jenna pulled Zoey around in a wobbly circle by both hands. Teenagers awkwardly kept their distance from each other under the watchful eyes of their parents.

Felicity was starting another session on the piano when Mercy, prompted by Kimberly, relented to taking a break. Mercy pulled a folding chair into the shadows near the corner of the Big Horn. Her unadulterated view of the party drifted with the haunting, unhurried melody. She rested her head against the barn wood and wondered how life in New York had ever appealed to her at all. There was a simplicity in Fayette she loved. The only hurry in town seemed to be in crop gathering or eating ice cream. She sighed and closed her eyes at the perfection of the moment, wrapped in Felicity's song.

Gravel crunched nearby and Mercy opened her eyes. Wyatt's tall figure could never be mistaken, even if he hadn't been wearing his cowboy hat. "Worked you to the bone?" he asked when he came within a few feet of her hiding spot.

Mercy sighed. His easygoing nature didn't intrude on her peace. "No. On a break and wanted to watch the dancing."

Wyatt's head swiveled back toward the canopy teeming with couples. The song changed but remained at a slow cadence. "So, how about a spin?" He turned back to Mercy and held out his hand.

Panicked, Mercy stammered. "I … don't … dance." Her eyes darted back and forth between his extended arm and his growing smile that she could barely make out from under the shadow of his hat.

"It's pretty easy. You hold onto me and I hold onto you and we spin in a circle, slowly." He took a step toward her chair. "That's why I asked during a slow song. With fast songs, I look like a baby horse learning to walk." Wyatt grabbed Mercy's hand and pulled her to her feet before she could decline again.

"Hang on," he said, placing both of his hands on her shoulders. "Let's lose the apron." Wyatt turned her around and untied the waist strings. Mercy stiffly lifted the apron over her head and tossed it to the chair. A big hand went to the small of her back and encouraged her forward movement toward the other dancing couples.

Once settled on the fringe of the crowd, Mercy did not glance up as she slid her left hand to his waist. Her breathing tempo galloped when he pulled her right hand to his chest. There were so many things to check out other than Wyatt's face—his tan shirt, the way her toes peeked out of the hem every so often, his trimmed beard, or the way he pressed her palm flat against his buttons so she could feel his heartbeat.

"You know, I've never danced with someone so interested in my boots," he said. She grinned and dared to drag her eyes up. "Come on, now. Am I so hideous?"

Her eyes fell to the crowd, and she met Adele's delighted smile. Mercy's heart plummeted, feeling desperately wrong, as if she were betraying her husband's memory. "No," she mumbled. "I just haven't danced since before Derrick died."

His hand held hers even tighter against his thumping heart. "I'm sorry. I didn't mean to joke about it." Wyatt's head had dropped, hat tilted sideways, and his lips were near her ear. "I'm so sorry, Mercy."

She simply nodded her head in reply, blinking back the tears, grateful his hat hid her face from half of the crowd. Mercy sniffed her nose into submission when he straightened.

"What is your favorite color?" he asked, nonchalantly.

The random question snapped Mercy's attention back to his face. "Um, blue? But not dark blue. Light blue."

His dark eyes twinkled. "Huh. I had you pegged for a green type of girl."

Mercy chuckled. It was easy to chat with him, no pretense necessary. "No. Not much green in the city." The faint odor of his cologne tickled her nose.

"Ah. Now you get to practice social civility and ask me what my favorite color is." Wyatt pressed and pulled her in a tight circle.

"I think you're a brown or tan guy. You know, man-of-the-earth, hunter and gatherer?"

"Aren't you a funny girl?" He jabbed a thumb near her waist.

"Not ticklish."

"Everyone is ticklish somewhere. And it's red."

"I'm not. And what type of red? Blood red? Or like the head of a woodpecker?" Mercy appreciated the way his eyebrows raced together at her questions. Jenna had pointed out a woodpecker to her the day before.

"How could you not be ticklish? You're an enigma. And woodpecker red is close enough. A nice bright red." His thumb still prodded her side.

"My rib cage will be bruised because of you." Mercy's mind scrambled for a safe question. "Would you rather fight a horse-sized duck or a hundred duck-sized horses?" Derrick loved to ask people that one.

Wyatt's laughter caused several heads to swivel their direction. His body bounced, and he drew Mercy closer to his chest. Once he finally caught his breath, he said, "I guess I'd go with the hundred duck-sized horses. Although, the horse-sized duck would make a fine meal."

"Of course you'd think about food," she said as the song ended and the crowd offered applause to the band.

Mercy clapped along, smiling as the band tipped their hats to the crowd. Wyatt bumped his arm sideways, causing her to take a step to the side. She recovered, wrinkled her nose and butted her shoulder into his bicep before walking back toward Kimberly.

Back behind the tables, Mercy had gathered dirty silverware into the basket when she realized her apron rested on the chair near the barn. She looked up just as a wad of material hit her chest. Wyatt grinned from the shadows as she flicked the apron open and covered her dress. Mercy smiled and grabbed the basket and a small stack of dirty plates. Her former dance partner retreated toward the crowd, which had begun to gather sleeping children and blankets.

Felicity's fingers danced along the ivory keys, a parting tune for the mass departure. Mercy kept busy shuttling dishes to the kitchen. Very little food was leftover. Kimberly had done a fantastic job organizing the entire event. By their comments, Mercy thought everyone who had come had enjoyed themselves as much as she had, despite her freezing toes. Adele waved Mercy over and the two shared a quick embrace before the older woman departed. Michael and Jenna encompassed her into a twin sandwich hug. Mercy squeezed back then returned to her clean-up duties.

Hank had filled one sink with soapy water at some point, so Mercy stood on the cement floor in the kitchen on her bare, dirty feet, and began the monumental task of cleaning dishes. She insisted Kimberly leave with her family. Hank, too. Mercy washed the dishes alone, careful to not drip onto the dress she had forgotten to change out of, humming an off-tune song Felicity had played.

A thought crept into her head slowly and all at once: it was good to feel again. It had been almost two years since Mercy had allowed herself to enjoy the moment, to savor the mood of happiness. Her shell of self-defense had cracked the moment Wyatt's warm hand pressed into the small of her back as he led her to dance. Elbow deep in soap bubbles, Mercy decided she would stop fighting joy.

"Thank you," she whispered out loud, because it was the only way she knew how to offer her first praise to God.

Chapter 6

By the time Mercy had drained the tepid water from the sink, her fingers were soggy and pruned. Her feet were numb from the cold cement floor, and she just wanted to go home and snuggle under her quilt. Mercy hung her apron near the back door. She decided to leave the dress on for the walk home to try and retain some of the magic of the party. Pulling on her socks and tennis shoes, she tucked her pants and shirt under an arm, turned off all of the lights, and pulled the locked door shut behind her.

Goosebumps broke out across her arms. A cold breeze pushed the long skirt against her ankles. Mercy contemplated pulling on her pants underneath the dress. Just as she shifted the pants from under her arm, a flashlight beam lit up her feet.

"Impeccable timing, Mrs. Benson," Wyatt's voice called from the other end of the light.

"If you didn't own the place, I'd call you a stalker," Mercy said, grateful she hadn't hiked up her skirts. "Why are you hanging out in the dark?"

Wyatt flipped the beam so it illuminated his face from under his chin. "Stalking." He could've seemed menacing if he hadn't smiled. The light returned to the ground before he continued. "Just finished packing up everything into the shed. Was just about to come in and make sure everything was all locked up when you interrupted my lurking in the shadows."

A freezing gust made Mercy tuck her hands under her arms. She could feel the cold settling into her bones and knew she had to be on her way. "I'll see you tomorrow."

"Today. It's almost two in the morning of tomorrow."

Mercy smiled. "Well then, I'll see you later today." As she stepped around Wyatt, she fished her own tiny flashlight out of the pocket of her folded pants. Her choice of not bringing her jacket proved to be a poor decision as she clasped her free hand over the tattoos on her lower arm. Her brain wondered if Wyatt would've been chivalrous enough to offer a jacket, had he been wearing one. She knew he didn't have one on. She remembered the soft texture of his faded tan shirt from their dance.

Mercy paused her retreat and glanced back to the cowboy who still stood near the kitchen door to the Big Horn. "Night, Boss," she called out. She resumed her path toward home.

Her smile slowly blossomed in the dark when his long stride sounded behind her and soon caught up. "Nice night for a walk."

She turned off her wimpy flashlight in favor of his brighter one. She tucked her elbows in close, as if to trap what little heat she radiated.

"I know you're cold, and I can see you don't have your jacket either. I'd offer to put my arm around you, but it probably would freak you out." Wyatt's admission rang true.

Mercy kept walking forward on the uneven pavement, eyes glued to the beam of light. Her mind warred with memories of Derrick and the new decision to enjoy life. In the end, necessity won.

"Okay." Her arms started to ache from the chill.

His warmth radiated through the material of the shirt as soon as he draped an arm across her shoulders and tucked her body closer to his own.

"You're freezing," he said, his hand rubbing her exposed arm.

Mercy was distracted by the nearness of Wyatt. She hummed a neutral response.

"So, light blue. Light blue like the chicken eggs or a clear, summer day?" His banter started as if they were still on the dance floor.

"Like a clear summer day. Too light and it reminds me of a hospital."

Even the warmth of his arms couldn't keep her nose from running. She sniffed, wishing for the hundredth time she had remembered to bring her jacket to pull over her nose.

"I'm sorry, I didn't mean to pry." Wyatt's palm squeezed her bicep.

It took a bit before Mercy understood. "No, I'm not crying. It's cold and my nose is running."

Wyatt chuckled. Mercy liked how easily he laughed. Derrick laughed all of the time, even when they were waking up the next morning after an all-night binge.

"Glad to hear it. Thought I had inadvertently dug myself another hole. I am quite proficient with putting my foot in my mouth."

Mercy shook her head in silent agreement.

"Tell me about your husband. I never got to meet my second cousin, and I've only heard bits and pieces from Heather. He may even be a third cousin, but I can't keep that all sorted. There are lots of us."

Mercy's feet kept walking, but her mind bounced like a hiccup.

"What exactly do you want to know?" She hoped he didn't want the details. She silently begged he just wanted the fluffy nothingness, like his name and how they met. No … hopefully just his name.

"All the sordid details. How did you meet?"

Of course. She dragged in a breath. "Uh, Derrick was at my friend's house the first time we met."

"Your eyes met across the room and boom! Love at first sight." His words brimmed with amusement.

"Not exactly," she said. Mercy knew their walk had at least ten more minutes and dreaded having asked for his arm around her, despite the warmth. "More like, he pulled me up from the floor where I had passed out."

"*Qué romantico!* Did he take you to the hospital?"

Anxiety made her skin prickle. "No. I was drunk."

Wyatt maneuvered his body to cross behind hers and warm up the opposite side. "That's not romantic at all. Unless you barfed on him." Mercy appreciated how he glossed over her embarrassment, but he didn't know the half of it.

"I never barfed afterwards." Killer headaches were her only telltale. She plunged on with her story before she chickened out. "We bonded over cheap alcohol. I was seventeen and he had a fake I.D. Mutual love of the bottle, I guess. But he was more than that…" Mercy's voice faded, lost in trying to recover Derrick's good qualities. "He was kind and funny. And I know it sounds cliché, but he was the only one who made me feel more than just some kid who hung out with whoever had food and booze."

"Did you hang out with whoever had food and booze?" Wyatt's tone sounded careful.

"Yup." She told him about her aunt and uncle who had passed her onto various distant relatives or friends throughout her life. "I was just a kid when my mom died. I don't even remember her. I felt like a burden to Auntie and Uncle. I lived from my suitcase, a week here, a month there. Had my first sip of home-stilled shine when I was fourteen. Felt like pure heaven to not have to think about where I was going or who I would stay with. It was fabulous to not worry or feel like a burden. I didn't feel anything at all." Mercy wished she had a bottle to ward off the quiet of sleeping Fayette as her admission tumbled out.

The rocks under their footsteps seemed to echo more loudly in the silence. Somewhere nearby, a dog barked. Every house slept in the dark.

"Derrick, though," Mercy continued a few steps later. "He caught on quick to my situation. His brother had just moved out, and he asked his mom if I could move in. Adele was not happy about the plan." She stopped and chuckled at the thought of Adele's crestfallen face when Derrick revealed his plan. "He said he would sleep on the couch and I could have his room. Oddly enough, Adele agreed. I still don't know what made her do it."

Mercy lost herself in reminiscing for a few moments. Adele had only lived with male companions in her household. The mother hen soon understood that Mercy valued her independence. "Adele was everything I had dreamed about for a mom. She made dinner every night. She packed lunches for Derrick, Christopher, and Papa Benson before they left for work. Laundry, dishes, cleaning house after working during the day as a bank teller. It was like moving in with someone from one of those black and white TV shows, except she didn't wear dresses."

"It's probably harder to wash laundry in dresses," Wyatt said. "I mean, not that I know from experience."

"I don't even think she owned a dress. Anyways, when she lost her job, I ended up taking a part-time job to help out. She taught me how to cook and tolerated the times I burnt something or messed up the soups." Mercy saw they passed the midway point of her route. "You know, I can walk the rest of the way by myself. It's not a big deal."

"And lose your personal jacket?" He scoffed. "Not a big deal. It's just a little ways away."

Mercy knew it was farther than "a little ways." He'd end up walking about twenty-five minutes back to his own house, as he lived just about five minutes from the Big Horn. While grateful for the heat Wyatt provided, Mercy hoped he would stop asking questions from her past. She liked their acquaintance just the way it was—the way he made sure to talk to her at work and church to make her feel less invisible. He didn't need to know too much about her history yet, or exactly how much she used to drink. Or how much she enjoyed the void drinking brought. She decided to shift the conversation.

"That was a great party tonight. Have you had one before?"

"This was the second one," he said. "The first one was last year, after the harvest, and we were able to throw something together before the weather turned. It looked nice because Felicity was in charge of the decorating." Wyatt's boot scuffed the asphalt. "I mean I *tried* to throw the party last year and that's why Kimberly organized it this time. We ran out of food, didn't have blankets for the hay bales for people to sit on, didn't have a band. Boring and miserable. I had to beg people to come this year." He kept the flashlight beam steady in front of her feet.

"I bet you didn't beg at all. You just made sure to tell them Kimberly ran it this time."

Again, he laughed. "Guilty. They know she runs a tight ship. I am so blessed to have her at the Big Horn. She was my mom's best friend, even though they were eleven years apart. And I only know because Kimberly likes to remind me she's *not* my mother's age."

"Yes, never ask a woman her age," Mercy said, steering clear of his mother. As much as she wanted to guard her past, she gave him the benefit of shielding his mom's memory.

"How old are you?" Wyatt asked.

"Twenty-two. You don't listen well."

"Never claimed to. I'm thirty-three."

"That's nice." Truth be told, Mercy already knew. Adele had told her, before dropping the fact that he'd been running the restaurant since his honorable discharge. They didn't discuss the scars on his face.

"What? No jokes about being a creepy, old stalker?"

"You're not *that* old. Just kinda old. Like, still-can-creep-in-the-shadows-since-you-don't-have-arthritis old." She paused. "However, you cannot creep, no matter your age, with your hat. It just doesn't scream 'stalker.'"

When he stopped walking, she halted too. Wyatt's hand left her arm and removed his hat. In the dim light that reflected back from the flashlight ahead of them, his dark hair matted down across his head. "Better?"

"No. Hat head is also not scary."

He replaced the hat as they neared Heather's house. "You're around back, right?" He steered them down the driveway.

"Yes." Mercy was a little disappointed to see her little home come into view. She enjoyed where the conversation headed toward the end of their walk, nothing guarded or tremendously meaningful. "Thank you for being my jacket," she murmured. "I don't think I'll ever forget to bring mine ever again."

She quickened her steps and unlocked the entry door. Looking back over her shoulder, she waved at Wyatt with her free hand before hurrying inside. Mercy pulled back the curtain on the door and waved again, tracking his flashlight beam as it turned toward the street.

The pain from her cold legs made her seek solace near the wall heater. The tiny flashlight appeared again so she didn't trip and wake Adele. She opened the refrigerator for a bottle of water, only to close it when the inside light turned on. Mercy stilled her movements and listened to Adele's breathing.

"I know you're not asleep," Mercy whispered to the older woman.

"Then why are you whispering?"

Mercy tiptoed to Adele's bed and sat on the edge near her mother-in-law's waist, flashlight pointed at the floor. "Because it's around two-thirty in the morning and it would be rude to talk at a normal speaking level." She tugged the edges of the blankets up out of habit, even though they were near Adele's chin. "What are you doing awake? Did you drink your chamomile tea?"

"Yes I did, but I just happened to wake up when you came in."

"Sorry I woke you." Mercy knew how difficult it was for Adele to sleep more than a few hours at a time. "Do you need anything before I go to bed?"

"Your dress is sure pretty." The pride in Adele's voice dropped her octave lower.

"Kimberly gave it to me," Mercy said. "She said she had saved it for her daughter, but she has her pack of boys." Mercy's hands, prickling as the warmth returned to them, smoothed out the flowered fabric across her lap. "I've never had a dress before."

"I never had one, either. Borrowed Heather's mom's to get married in. I think that dress had been in three or four weddings by the time I got my turn." Adele described her borrowed wedding dress in a hushed voice, reverent and full of emotion. Fayette had been turned upside down with gossip when Adele and Henry were married by the local judge the weekend after they met in a whirlwind romance.

Mercy asked Adele if she'd like another cup of tea. Somewhere in the story of Adele's wedding dress, Mercy's mind decided to fully wake again, and she knew she'd only toss and turn on the sofa bed. When Adele agreed, Mercy turned on the lamp. Without asking, she unwrapped some zucchini bread and sliced two pieces, leaning them against the kettle to warm while Adele sat up in bed. She placed the bread onto napkins, pulled the hot water off of the stove, and poured the first cup.

"That was nice of Wyatt to walk you home."

Mercy nearly dropped the kettle.

"I … I didn't know you heard him." Like a child who'd been caught licking the frosting off of a birthday cake, Mercy silently chided herself. Wyatt was only her boss: funny, no drama, and had someone else interested in him. Felicity fit him perfectly, which made it safe to be his friend.

"I thought I heard you two talking. He's a thoughtful young man." Mercy could hear the hope, the encouragement, in Adele's voice.

"He's my boss," Mercy countered, voice low and even. The tea steeped, and she stirred the spoon with a bit more vigor than needed. The last thing she needed was her own mother-in-law pushing her into the arms of another man. "I am still in love with Derrick," she added, for a sense of complete explanation.

"Derrick only ever wanted you to be happy."

Mercy didn't have the right words to rebuke Adele's statement. Derrick always reminded her it was his goal to make her laugh. And with the memory of her husband's promise, her heart longed for him again.

No, she wouldn't be over Derrick for a long time.

Adele finished her tea and bread, then Mercy helped her back under the blankets. She refused to respond to the older woman's honest observation. It was easier to put the thoughts of the dance and walk home into a nice corner in her mind and leave them there.

In the bathroom, Mercy changed out of her dress. She washed her face in the chilly water and thought about the time Derrick had woken her by throwing water on her. She pulled out the sofa bed and remembered when he'd haul her intoxicated body home by the hand.

When she slid under the cool comforter, lost in between memories and sleep, the loneliness wrapped her tight against its chest.

Chapter 7

The first thing Mercy saw when she woke the next morning was the green dress hanging from the curtain rod next to the sofa bed. It dangled limp and shadowed. She reached her hand out from under the covers and pushed the smooth fabric between her fingers.

She and Adele dressed for church, Mercy foregoing the dress in favor of her clean khaki pants. They walked across the driveway for breakfast with the Kinnetts. Robert met them at the dining room door, then pulled out chairs around the table for them. Michael chatted about basketball try-outs, and Jenna repeated her request at least twice for new rainboots. Mercy volunteered to walk to church after eating, because the huge truck was squished to capacity. When Robert offered to walk with her, she nodded her agreement.

He pulled his baseball cap low after following her down the driveway. "How are you liking Fayette so far?" His breath curled into the air.

"I like it."

"And how's it going at the Big Horn?"

Mercy pulled her jacket zipper up as high as it would go and stuffed her hands into the pockets. "It's good. Happy to get a paycheck." And food. But she wouldn't admit that to him.

Robert paced his steps with hers. "Glad that all worked out. Wyatt's a good guy. He's always busy."

She didn't respond, burrowing her chin into the collar of her coat. Wyatt stopped by the Big Horn every day—sometimes he stayed until she called out good night and locked the doors. Those nights, he frowned over numbers.

They approached a faded stop sign with a piece of peeling duct tape, the rusted bolts leaving copper colored trails between the "T" and the "O." Robert actually glanced both ways, despite the lack of cars. "I'm headed down to Redding later, if you want to come."

"No, thank you. It's my day off and I want to spend some time with Adele." She didn't want him to get any ideas that she was interested. He was practically her cousin by marriage.

"It's great how well you two get along."

The cold air froze Mercy's nose as she inhaled. "She's my family."

"Yeah, Heather told me how … I mean … sorry. I know you probably don't want to talk about it."

The house church had never been so exciting to see until that moment. No one spent time lingering in the cold this morning. Mercy sped up to flee the conversation.

Wyatt was already on the porch and held the door open. "Let me guess, keeping your jacket."

She grinned and ducked inside, searching for Adele. Mercy stood behind her mother-in-law, like she always did, and sang along with one of the songs. Her hands pulled into tight fists when Pastor Ron started.

"Does anyone here have an unforgivable sin? Something they'd never tell anyone else?"

Mercy was sure that everyone in the room focused on her, but she kept her unblinking gaze on the pastor while he continued. She desperately tried to make sense about a God who would forgive past sins and give a person hope for the future. It was everything she wanted, but couldn't possibly be meant for her ears. Her sins, her past, were more than anyone in the room, including Adele, could ever forgive.

When everyone left church, Mercy stayed glued to Adele's elbow, occasionally glancing around. Wyatt carried Zoey in one arm while she played with his earlobe. Robert stood with a group of older men next to Wyatt. She couldn't hear what they were saying, but they all frowned and nodded while listening to each other speak.

A whistle pierced the noise. Mercy cringed, and the small children slapped their hands over their ears. Pastor Ron stood on a folding chair, clasping onto Robert's shoulder for balance. "I almost forgot to tell you the great news! The permit is finalized and we are going to start pouring the foundation next week!"

Ear-splitting applause and shouts echoed on the high ceilings.

"In celebration, and to get more volunteers," Pastor Ron said, smiling to those who laughed, "we are going to have a picnic next Saturday at the Big Horn, so I'll see you there!"

Mercy glanced at Wyatt, who whispered something to Zoey. Even knowing the amount of work she'd have to do, Mercy anticipated another chance to wear her dress. This time, she'd wear shoes to keep her toes from freezing.

Wyatt called out to Mercy as she helped Adele into Heather's truck. "You okay with working the extra hours?"

"Yeah, sure." She'd cashed her previous paychecks, and tucked the cash under the kitchen sink. The prospect of opening a checking account at the only bank in Fayette thrilled her, but she kept her excitement tamped down.

"Perfect. Kimberly already ordered the hog, and I'm sure she'll fill you in tomorrow."

"Okay, thanks."

Adele cleared her throat and reached for the door handle. "See you at home?"

"I'll be there soon." Mercy stepped back as the engine roared to life. The sun warmed her back when she turned to walk home.

"Want some company?" Wyatt stepped next to her on the shoulder of the road.

"I think Robert is coming."

His face puckered, and he rubbernecked behind them. "There he is. I need to talk with him about the fields anyways."

The trio headed back toward the Kinnett house. The guys prattled on about crop rotation and combine maintenance. Mercy counted the crows, not understanding a word but thankful she didn't have to contribute to the conversation.

"See you in the morning, Boss." Robert clapped Wyatt's hand in a shake and then went into the big house.

"You're his boss, too?"

Wyatt shrugged. "Yeah. He works on the farm side of my businesses."

"Businesses. As in many?"

"Technically, six."

"You sound important." Her eyebrows arched high and she fought to keep from grinning.

"I could be, to the right person." He half-turned to leave, his eyes never leaving hers. "See you tomorrow."

"Okay, Boss."

Mercy entered her home and found a beat-up cardboard box on the small dining table. Adele poured a cup of tea. "Heather said the kids found this up in the attic. I mentioned that I missed crocheting." Funny how many things were found in the Kinnett's attic.

Inside the box, a jumble of yarn sat in a pile. Mercy and Adele pushed the colorful threads back and forth to survey their prize. Mercy moved the box onto the floor and settled next to it while her mother-in-law remained on the slightly more comfortable couch. Each took turns reaching in to remove a skein or wad, carefully separating the decades-old yarn. Once they emptied the box, they were surrounded by vivid mounds, and Adele wanted some semblance of order.

"Let's get these rolled into balls so they don't tangle when we put them back in."

Mercy agreed, taking the nearest jumble to task.

"Are you going to talk about the elephant in the room?"

"Huh?" Mercy fumbled with the knotted mess in her lap.

"About Wyatt. He's been such a gentleman."

Slowly blinking, she blew a frustrated sigh through her nose, annoyed by the suggested candidate for a boyfriend she didn't want or need. "Sounds like you want to talk about it."

"Don't get miffed at me. You keep walking around like you're oblivious to the whole situation."

"I'm not oblivious." Mercy yanked the yarn in her hands. "I don't see Wyatt like that. He's my friend, my boss. I just don't understand why even you can't see it. We are friends. Period."

"His decision or yours?" Adele's question hung in the air while her hands purposefully spun yarn into a green ball.

"Does it matter?"

"Mercy." Adele exhaled. "Child, if you could see the way he watches you."

"I don't want him to watch me that way. We are *friends.*" She finished a small sphere of black and moved toward a pile of brown. "Besides, Felicity is already interested in him. And it's what makes our friendship just perfect. We don't have to pretend to be friends because we like each other." Even as Mercy's words came, they tasted wrong.

"You don't sound so sure of yourself."

"I am." Certainly, the more times she said and thought those words, the more natural it would feel.

"As long as you're sure of it, I'll leave it be."

Mercy could see the disappointment in Adele's eyes. Wyatt was everything a woman could hope for as a husband for her own daughter—kind, handsome, and far above the meager lives that they lived. Adele offered a smile of encouragement, but Mercy reminded herself of the reasons why Wyatt would pity and, eventually, despise her. Nobody wanted to be saddled with a broke, recovering-alcoholic widow, with years of guilt over her husband's death.

Mercy moved to untangle another mess of yarn. She concentrated on the ends and colors, pulling the right one through tangles. "I'm sure," she said, with as much resolve as she could muster.

The pair moved in silence, rolling balls of all sizes and colors before depositing them back into the box. When they finished, Mercy asked her mother-in-law for a crochet refresher. She hadn't touched any yarn since long before they left New York, back when the family had lived together.

Adele thumbed through the handful of metal crochet hooks from the box and picked out a faded blue one. She offered a similar one to Mercy.

Side by side, Mercy mirroring her mentor, the pair worked the hooks through the yarn until each had mastered a simple chain stitch. Each pulled the string taunt. Hoops disappeared into a single strand again before creating another chain.

They took a break and ate leftovers for dinner before returning to their elementary work. Adele looped yarn over the top of the hook and pulled it through a hoop and repeated her motion. Mercy watched, confused. Adele repeated her movements, singing through the action like a child's song: "Loop one, pull two. Loop one, pull one."

After Mercy turned on another light and each had a blanket around their legs for warmth, she soon completed her first imperfect row of stitches. Still held in her hands, the trail of uneven yarn stretched to her feet.

Adele had fallen back into the memory of crocheting and steadily worked her needle and multicolored yarn in a small square. "Pot holder," she said with a smile, turning the four-sided piece one way and then the other. Adele turned her attention back to her craft after instructing Mercy how to turn the stitch at the end of the row.

When Adele excused herself to go to bed because her eyes were tired, Mercy plugged away, looping and drawing the yarn through. Lost in concentration of getting the tension of the yarn correct, the end of the skein caught her by surprise. She tied it to a nearby stitch and wove the loose end in. Wrapping the blue lopsided scarf around her throat, Mercy stood up to catch her reflection in the window above the sink. She let down her bun and thought about the dance, wondering if Wyatt would compliment her handiwork, before banishing the thought back into its corner.

Giddy from her successful, yet ugly, scarf, Mercy rummaged through the yarn box again, pulling out the softest fibers her fingers touched. A hodgepodge of various colors, she arranged them in a rainbow-inspired color pallet from red through purple then to black. She stashed the velvety yarns into the back of her dresser drawer, then inched out the squeaky sofa bed. Out of habit, she made the small circuit of the tiny house, checking the windows and door locks.

Mercy squinted at the calendar tacked near the doorway. Her finger dragged along the boxes, counting the days. With a smile, she turned off the light and climbed into her own bed.

She had exactly ninety-eight days to figure out how to crochet Adele a shawl for Christmas.

***

The groaning hinges of the Big Horn's back kitchen door invaded the golden silence of the following afternoon, just after the breakfast crowd had departed. Felicity called out a friendly hello. Mercy nodded her head, eyes glued to the weeds between the lines of onions. She knew Felicity probably wore something meticulous and beautiful while Mercy groveled in holey jeans and an oversized sweatshirt to ward off the chill.

"I can't believe you garden without gloves!" Felicity spread a towel on the ground inches from Mercy's spot to protect her black pants. She tugged on a dainty pair of leather gloves before she plucked weeds with more grace than the ice skaters at the Rockefeller Center rink.

"I don't use them," Mercy mumbled.

"Don't need gloves if you like to get your hands dirty." Wyatt appeared near the greenhouse and knelt across the row from Mercy, his hat shielding his face when he spoke.

"Sure, but it's harder to scrub out from under your nails," Felicity said in an impossibly melodic voice.

Mercy just wanted to finish her task in silence but knew it wouldn't happen with the addition of two more in the garden. She examined the row she needed to finish, then the pumpkin plants that Hank told her needed to be pulled from the ground. Here in the garden, before her serenity had evaporated, she was useful. Now, she morphed into the third wheel. She moved away from Felicity and down the row.

"You should get a haircut." Mercy peered up to see Felicity pulling one of Wyatt's brown curls at his neck through her fingers.

Mercy swallowed her rebuttal. Wyatt didn't need a haircut. Besides, the brown, lazy curls were downright appealing when they peeked out from under his cowboy hat. She snorted at the idea of Wyatt cutting his hair simply because Felicity had made the idea.

"You think so?" He leveled his eyes at Mercy over the onions.

She squinted and shook her head, returning to the weeds. Such a pushover.

"Oh yes. It looks so much better when it's short. Don't you think, Mercy?"

Mercy wanted nothing to do with the decision, no matter if his longer hair made her belly squirm. "I don't care one way or the other. As long as he doesn't grow a billy-goat of a beard again." She lobbed a small clod of dirt in his direction before moving farther away.

"I kinda liked the beard." Felicity sounded hurt at the suggestion.

"You didn't have to clean it." Mercy scoffed and instantly regretted doing so.

"You cleaned his beard?"

Mercy didn't have to lift her eyes. In his lack of response, Mercy could practically hear Wyatt's smile as she tried to figure out a delicate way to answer and not offend the woman at his side.

"I do *not* recommend it," Mercy finally said.

"When did you do that?" Felicity's voice pitched up, as if she had more to say and cut of the end of her thoughts.

Knowing there would be no end until Felicity was satisfied with the details, Mercy gave a condensed version.

"My first day of work. He got taffy into it and then had paint on his hands and couldn't clean it. Honestly, it was just a favor." She celebrated a small mental victory as she surveyed his shorter beard.

No need to reveal to Felicity that Mercy had allowed her thoughts to dwell on Wyatt as more than her friend every so often. Mercy worked on moving the bucket down toward the pumpkin plants, away from the man who surely stared at her.

"If you come over later, I can cut off your hair and we can talk about bringing your beard back," Felicity said, in a higher tone not meant for Mercy.

"Well, we can *talk* about a haircut. I haven't made up my mind yet."

Mercy turned her shoulder to hide her smile. A clump of dirt hit her shin. If Felicity were more amiable, and Mercy less petrified at the reaction, Mercy would've chucked the contents of her bucket at Wyatt. Instead, she peeked over her shoulder at the grinning gargoyle in a cowboy hat.

Chapter 8

A couple of days later, Wyatt coerced Mercy to walk to the nearby pond behind the Big Horn between the breakfast and dinner crowds. They tromped through the underbrush, Mercy stepping into his big boot treads in order to avoid snakes. His version of a "pond" was a lake in her opinion.

"How did Derrick die?"

Wyatt's unexpected question deflated Mercy into shame. She instinctively took a step back as her breathing sped up.

Mercy didn't answer right away. She didn't even move, other than to breathe, keeping her eyes on her scuffed boots. She'd never had anyone outright ask her about Derrick's death. Normally, people would dance around the topic, carefully trying to ask the "right" questions to glean tidbits. While she wanted to tell Wyatt, and appreciated his forthright approach, the words were buried under years of practiced refusal.

"I'm not sorry I asked," he said, taking a step away from her and toward the shoreline. He leaned over and chucked a rock into the water. The ripples settled flat before he spoke again. "Maybe someday you'll tell me. Maybe not."

Mercy scanned the water, the weight of Wyatt's revelation bogging her mind down. She didn't understand why, but she knew she needed to tell him. "I'm not good at talking about it," she stammered to his back.

"Would it make it easier if I stare at the pond while you talk?"

"Yes."

Wyatt sat on the dirt. When she made no sound, he threw another stone. It plunked into the water.

"I was very drunk that night," Mercy began, humiliation flooding her cheeks with heat. "There weren't very many nights we weren't drunk." She paused, deciding whether she should go backwards in her story, or just plow through the details of that night. "I told you before how we both had a mutual love of the bottle."

"I remember how you met," he said, twirling a small stick between his thumbs.

Mercy inhaled sharply. "We had a blow-out fight. He wanted a baby so badly and I ... the thought made me sick." She recounted the memories that were fuzzy: drinking at a friend's, the argument over her doctor's appointment the next day that spilled onto the street when they left.

"It's spotty from there. I remember yelling. He was so mad at me for drinking when I thought I might be pregnant." She picked at her cuticles until they bled.

"Looking back now, I'm mad at myself for it. I kinda remember running across the street to get away from him. Derrick was still yelling on the other side and then it got quiet, so I turned around. I know from the doctor's report that he fell, got clipped by a car, and died of a brain trauma. I didn't even hear the car or impact. But I do remember all of the blood. A *lot* of blood.

"I just remember blood and screaming. His eyes were open and his mouth kept opening and closing. Then, the hospital." She shivered at the memory, the tang smell of sterility and beeping monitors. Mercy had awoken to her mother-in-law rubbing a circular pattern on her palm.

"Adele didn't even have to tell me about Derrick. I knew by her face, because she'd already looked that way with Papa Benson and Christopher. But, she did have to tell me about the baby." Adele's heartbreak crushed Mercy, who fought through the haze of medications to understand everything her mother-in-law explained. Mercy *had* been pregnant. The doctors said that it was probably a combination of the alcohol and stress, but they weren't sure.

At the pause in her recollection, Wyatt swiveled his body toward her. Exhausted by her story, Mercy sat down in the dirt across from his extended legs. A glance up from her dirty jeans confirmed that he studied her. Relief flooded her, like a simultaneous warm blanket from the dryer, followed by a face full of ice water. The story was out. And now he could hate her as much as she hated herself.

"I'd taken away the last things dear to her. Every last hope." Mercy choked on her words, swiping at the tears as they fell. She regarded the water over Wyatt's shoulder. Now that her secret laid bare before him, she could accept his verdict. And it made her feel as peaceful as the calm pond. Finally, someone else knew her wretched life. She only wished that he'd still be her friend, or at least say hello once in a while.

Wyatt scoffed, and Mercy's gaze snapped to him.

"You want me to condemn you, Mercy Benson. You want to be beaten over the head with your past." He narrowed his eyes.

She hoisted her chin up a tic, tears starting again. "I can barely live with what I did."

"You choose not to allow yourself happiness and keep everyone at a distance."

"Sometimes. It's safer that way."

Mercy prepared herself to guard her belief: being alone left no room for heartbreak or more guilt. But as her mind flipped into prepared responses, Wyatt remained quiet and turned his own attention back to the water, uncharacteristically silent.

His jaw muscles clenched under his beard before he released a deep sigh. When he reached a hand up from the ground and rubbed the back of his neck, Mercy refused to give into the longing to scoot over and massage it for him.

Instead, she offered an explanation. "I'm not lonely. I have Adele and you." She forced a small smile when he focused on her. "Kimberly and Hank.

Being alone and being lonely are two different things and I'm okay with being alone. It's just better for me."

"That's a lame excuse."

Mercy's head jerked back. "What?"

"You want friendship on your terms. You use your husband's death as a convenient excuse to thumb your nose at what God has put right in front of you."

Anger bubbled past her sorrow. "And what exactly has God put in front of me?" Her voice shook with fury. How dare he throw Derrick's death in her face?

"Do you have to ask?" He hoisted his body up, stared down at her. Jaw working behind his shortened beard, he turned and disappeared down the path.

As sure as the sensation of warmth returning to her cold hands, it dawned on Mercy that Wyatt meant himself. He literally stood right in front of her and she had used her excuses to deflect him.

As a mockingbird warbled its stolen songs, she wrestled with her past, with Derrick. Pastor Ron's words came back to her in sporadic parts: "I confessed my sins and Jesus forgave them." Mercy's condemnation had pummeled her ears when the words were spoken—she was the one with unforgivable sin. But seated in the dirt, conviction weighted her shoulders with the loss of Derrick and their child. And she knew she needed to move forward with her life, like Adele had. She couldn't change the past. Derrick would never come back.

When it grew dark and crickets replaced the birds, Mercy finally hauled herself from the shoreline. She wanted to find Wyatt, but her feet pulled her to the Big Horn's kitchen, where Hank took one look at her and told her to take the night off. She shuffled home, knowing it would be empty. Adele was playing cards at a friend's after dinner. They would bring her home around eight.

Leo the cat darted out from near the main house as Mercy unlocked the door, sneaking into the guest home. She moved through the room in darkness. Ignoring the rumbling in her stomach, Mercy lugged the sofa bed out and flopped onto the mattress. Haphazardly throwing the blankets over her fully dressed frame, her unsteady breathing gave way to tears and then sobs.

"I have nothing to give him," she whispered to the cat, as it walked across her reclining body.

He had Felicity.

***

Mercy knelt in the garden in the waning dusk. The smell of the sun-warmed dirt mingled with the distinct hint from the ripe onions. She didn't know when it had happened, but the aroma now signaled a sense of purpose. Moving the stalks to pull weeds, she checked for ripeness. The methodical task let her mind wander back to the day before, when Wyatt had revealed his heart and she, like a moron, had bumbled the whole thing.

To crush her mental debate, Mercy tried to hum the melody from the song the previous Sunday. When her memory of the tune failed, she chose a song she knew—the song she had danced to with Wyatt. Plucking a giant, red onion from its hill, Mercy swallowed the unexpected thought of … love. She certainly didn't deserve a guy like Wyatt. Adele's encouragement didn't help either. Why didn't either of them see the massive faults in her life? Or her struggle to understand Pastor Ron's words about hope and forgiveness? How could they forgive her past?

She reached the end of the onions and moved toward the chard when she heard the kitchen door. Mercy didn't turn. She didn't want to see Wyatt's judgement in his drawn face, or the way he would turn and leave. Instead, she kept her eyes on her hands as she turned the leaves, searching for aphids or cutworms, like Hank had shown her.

Right up until Wyatt's work boots stopped on the opposite side of the row, inches from her hands.

Smothering a breath of panic, Mercy rocked back to her heels and pondered her boss—the man who had been honest when no one else dared mention Derrick's name. He stared at her from under his hat, hazel eyes resolute.

"Hi." Mercy's voice wavered, betraying her scattered mind.

"Hey." Wyatt's voice was as steady as his gaze.

When his conversation failed to proceed and her neck ached, Mercy moved her attention back to the chard. "I want to finish this row before it gets dark," she blurted, immediately regretting her words. Avoiding the inconvenient truth in the onion row appeared to be her specialty.

Wyatt's boots turned toward the Big Horn.

"Wait!" Mercy toppled over in her haste to make the situation right. A big hand extended near her face.

She took his warm, calloused palm.

"I'm sorry about yesterday," she said, once upright.

"Are you saying that to garner sympathy or are you going to quit making excuses?"

Mercy sucked in a breath while her mind scrambled for an answer. "It's what I'm used to doing. I'm good at excuses. Grew up making them to get by and it is easy to do." She noticed he still held her grubby hand in his and refrained from pulling it away. "I *am* sorry." Her eyes remained on their hands, hoping she wouldn't sniff and give away her emotions.

"We all have a past. There's a saying that I live by, because I have a past, too. I wasn't the same guy you see right now. 'You are more than the mistakes you've made.' That was the last thing my mom wrote to me, followed by a Bible verse."

"Which verse?"

"Second Corinthians, chapter twelve, verse nine."

Mercy waited for Wyatt to recite the verse, but shifted her eyes to his face when he remained quiet. His eyes were closed. His silence made her fidget. He usually had an answer for everything. A slow smile spread just before he squinted at her.

"You'll have to look it up."

She had no reply other than to swallow past the lump in her throat. Mercy pulled her hand from Wyatt's and mumbled that she needed to take the onion to storage. What she needed was to be alone to think about what he had said—being more than her past.

"Mercy," Wyatt hollered, stopping her just as she reached for the kitchen door.

She looked across the garden, remembering when he had said he was right in front of her. Who had told her she was more than her mistakes. The same man who now tipped his cowboy hat as the sun dipped behind the horizon.

"I don't give up. It's not in my nature to quit."

Mercy's smile blossomed wide and her free arm crushed the onion stalks close, releasing their pungent scent. She wanted to say she was glad for his fight, but the words dammed up behind embarrassment. Instead, she nodded and fled into the kitchen, grateful to disappear into the cool storage room.

Hank must have heard her entrance and came to feast his eyes on the onion she laid on the back shelf. He rattled off the menu recipes for the following day, making a check mark in the air with his finger as he passed the necessary ingredients.

When the pair returned to the kitchen, Mercy washed up before tying on her apron to help Hank with the dishes. She nearly dropped the plate she was drying when Felicity's ringing laughter came through the doors to the restaurant. Where Felicity held court, Wyatt was sure to be near. Mercy didn't mind seeing him again, but the thought of him with Felicity or hearing Felicity laugh at his jokes, or putting her dainty hand on his arm? All of it made Mercy clench her jaw. She set the plate down with more force than she had intended.

Hank noticed. "Didn't think much got under your skin."

Mercy swiveled toward the cook, who kept his eyes on the sink full of dishes. "Well, sometimes … things do."

"Didn't say that it was a bad thing, neither."

His response prompted her smile. Suddenly, she didn't mind Felicity's melodic voice as much and returned to the benign task at hand. Dinner hastened the night while Mercy steered the conversation with Hank toward the greenhouse and growing vegetables for the winter. They chattered until Kimberly came into the kitchen and plopped the last fork down.

"You'd think it's the holidays with all the visitors in town," she sighed. "I need to train another one of you, kid." Kimberly pinched Mercy's cheek. "Or be able to sprout more arms."

"Give me a sec and I'll be out to clean up. Why don't you go home to your boys? Hank, I can finish up. No need to keep the both of you." Mercy tucked a loose strand of hair behind her ear.

She straightened her apron with a grin when both heeded her orders. Kimberly called out that the doors were locked and Hank yawned his goodnight. Mercy finished in the kitchen, then she drained the water to the greenhouse and moved to the dining hall.

She cranked up the radio next to the cash register and turned half of the lights off to conserve energy. Kimberly always laughed at the leftover "city" habit. Mercy wiped down the tables and chairs, one by one, before flipping the chairs to the clean tabletops. Her broom swept in time with the jazz music.

The back door squeaked open, Mercy froze mid-dance with the mop. Had she forgotten to lock it? Her grip tightened on the mop until Wyatt appeared near the radio. She sighed.

"You scared the bejeezus out of me!"

"Sorry. Heard the music and saw the lights. Didn't mean to interrupt you." A lazy smile crept up his lips.

Mercy's cheeks burned. "Were you watching me?"

"Watching you what?"

"Dance."

"Dance with who?"

"With my mop."

"What?" Wyatt's eyebrows pulled together. Mercy was torn between figuring out if he was teasing her or really didn't see her swaying to the music.

"Never mind," she said.

"No, no. You were dancing with your mop?"

She shoved the cleaning implement back and forth once more, trying to ignore the mirth in his voice and her scorching face.

"First a duster, now a mop," Wyatt continued. "Your dance partners are horrible at conversation. I'll dance with you."

"I gotta finish mopping."

"Yeah, I heard your boss is a real slave driver."

Mercy narrowed her eyes at the joker in the kitchen doorway. She knew he would be as persistent as the blackberry stain on her apron. "You'll have to wait your turn. These floors won't clean themselves. There's no mop fairy."

"Shocking. Then who has been taking the cookies I leave out?"

"Go away and let me mop!" She laughed as he sulked toward the office.

At last, Mercy retreated to the kitchen to rinse the mop and empty the bucket. Anticipation burrowed into nervousness when she thought of everything that had happened between her and Wyatt in the past few days. She performed her tasks slowly, hoping in equal parts that he would pop into the doorway or not appear, having fallen asleep at his desk. As she hung up her apron on the hook, his deep voice made her jolt.

"Is the cleaning fairy all done?"

"I don't have wings," Mercy said. "You don't have to dance with me. I smell like dirty dishes." She wanted him to agree, just this once.

"And you have dirty kneecaps too, so let's do this." Wyatt pushed through the swinging door and grabbed her wrist. She protested until they were facing each other, hand in hand.

"We both can't dance to fast music." Mercy remembered his comment from the harvest party.

"It's okay. We'll be ridiculous together." They giggled their way through several dances. Mercy stepped on Wyatt's feet, and he on hers. Somewhere along the line, she realized several songs had gone by.

"What time is it?" she asked.

"Do you have a curfew?"

"Would you care?"

"What if I did?" His hat removed, the irises in his eyes were blown wide open from the lowered lights.

"Are we answering in questions?"

"Do you want to play that game?"

"Do you think you could actually win?" She smirked.

Before she had time to react, Wyatt leaned forward and gently kissed her. "Yup."

"Cheater." She curled her lips together, as if to capture his kiss.

He grinned. "Not a bad way to lose."

Chapter 9

Mercy couldn't help grinning as she put her green dress on again for the church party. A spark of memory reminded her of her dance with Wyatt, her "personal jacket," before she dashed the thought away. She remembered to grab her own coat before leaving this time.

Mercy arrived just as Kimberly's two oldest boys were bringing out tables from the Big Horn, little hands gripping the table that teetered with their small steps.

"They're almost teenagers and know everything. They've got it handled," Kimberly assured Mercy when it nearly tipped.

The women retrieved the food and plates in numerous trips to and from the tables and kitchen. Between the deliveries, Mercy caught sight of Wyatt moving in and out of the shed, arms laden with chairs and decorations. Felicity arrived soon after Mercy, dressed in a fantastic, flowing concoction of oranges and reds. The splash of bright colors flitted around the area, stringing ribbons and lights, laughing and breaking into random songs. Mercy tried not to feel inadequate wearing her recycled dress.

Wyatt lifted his chin when they crossed paths. She couldn't help but smirk at the longer beard he sported. It sprang out in all directions, unkept and wiry. He claimed to be growing it out for the winter, along with his hair, so that he "didn't get cold," as he explained after he'd walked her home the night before.

"You don't get cold! You were my jacket."

"Yes, I was your jacket, but you haven't had a full Fayette winter yet. And this year is supposed to be a doozy. Colder temperatures and more snow than the last few years."

"Way to sell it, Boss." Mercy mentally made a note to finish crocheting her double layer cap and try to make a pair of mittens.

He delivered the chairs and helped Felicity with a strand of ribbons. They were perfect together, the way Felicity leaned into Wyatt to show him where to tack the line. Then Wyatt laughed at something Felicity said. Mercy turned away, remembering the fleeting kiss he'd given her. Maybe it was out of sympathy. Cutlery waited to be rolled into napkins.

Kimberly moved to the fire pit that had been built near the chow line and called for Mercy to help. Next to the coals, buckets of pumpkin slices floated in salt water. The two women lowered a cooking grill to rest above the heat. As they drained the water to the ground, Mercy caught a glimpse of Wyatt and Hank moving the pig from the underground barbeque where it had been cooking in all day.

Maple syrup was drizzled over the damp pumpkin slices before they were lined up like soldiers on the grill. "I forgot the nutmeg," Kimberly said, sending Mercy to the Big Horn.

She ran her finger across the enormous spice bottles in an open cupboard near the stove when Wyatt came in through the back door. "Need any help?" He moved close, but didn't touch her.

"I just need to get the nutmeg for Kimberly."

"Here." He reached to the top shelf and pulled it down for her.

"Thank you."

"Of course." He didn't move, blocking her path to the door.

Mercy forced herself to look up. He did that weird thing Derrick used to do: bouncing from one foot to the other, back and forth, like he was trying to get ready to say something.

"Could you love me?"

Wyatt's face held a combination of seriousness and hope—eyebrows up and breath held. Mercy stilled, unsure she had heard his words correctly. The tips of her fingers were icy cold when he pulled the nutmeg away and wrapped them into his warm hands.

"Mercy?" His voice tilted with expectation.

"What about Felicity?" She babbled the first thing that came to mind.

"What about her?" Wyatt sounded perplexed by her response.

Mercy dropped her eyes from Wyatt's face to their hands. He had surrounded her smaller ones with his own. Panic toyed with her thoughts. She wanted this, to feel love and be enough for someone like him. But he would probably change his mind and she'd be truly alone. Again.

"I thought…"

"No." His cowboy hat slowly shook back and forth while his hands clutched hers. "What about Robert?" His question dripped with sarcasm.

Mercy screwed her face together. "Ew. No. He's Heather's brother. I barely know him. But Felicity is perfect for you."

"I'm a tad confused. Why you are arguing for another woman when I just asked you that question?"

Her palms started to quiver. "I don't want anything to change." Mercy was trapped under a landslide of doubt. Tears fell as quickly as they formed. "You don't know me. You'll hate me."

Wyatt's face slackened. "I know what you tell me. I know who you are now."

"Please, please don't ask me that, Wyatt. I am just your friend. I don't know how to love anymore. I'm broken."

His silence spoke volumes. When he pulled his hands from hers, Mercy wanted to take them back and try to explain that she just wasn't the right one for him, that Felicity had so much more to offer. Her mind shrieked to tell him that she was petrified of loving again, being left alone again. But she stood unmoving, staring at his back as he walked out of the door.

Mercy retrieved the nutmeg and loped back to Kimberly. She wanted to keep walking into the dark woods and disappear. She wanted to find Wyatt and apologize for being scared and lying. She wanted to be happy.

She wanted to be happy with Wyatt.

Instead, she kept her gaze to the food and ground. Anywhere but to her heart's desire.

The activity became her focus. The pork was shuttled to the serving table and piled into bowls. Kimberly's boys brought out the sliced loaves of bread from the kitchen while their mother flipped the pumpkin and seasoned the other side with the nutmeg. Mercy's stomach begged for a morsel as families arrived and heaped their plates.

Mercy's misery only grew when the dancing started and Felicity crooned love songs from the stage. Out of the corner of her eyes, Mercy could see Wyatt peer over the rim of his glass of water toward her as she wiped the tables clean. She could sense that he wanted to ask her something and she knew that if she kept busy, he wouldn't interrupt or make a scene.

Her solitude sank its inky fingers farther down, strangling the notion of a happily ever after.

Pastor Ron sidled up to her. "How's it going, Mercy?"

She nodded, thinking her mute response would make him move along. It did. But in his wake, the thoughts of forgiveness and hope waged their own war against her despair.

Mercy tried not to notice Wyatt throughout the night—the way he pulled little Zoey into his arms and danced with over-exaggerated movements. Or when he came through the chow line to make sure everything was okay. It took a monumental amount of self-control for Mercy to not glimpse around after the piano fell silent, knowing Felicity would be on a path toward Wyatt. But when she did work up the nerve to sneak a peek, every part of her body warmed when he pointedly met her gaze and walked away from Felicity before they could even speak.

He wanted her to see his choice, even after she'd messed up. Again.

It gnawed at Mercy's mind, the push and pull of daring to embrace happiness, as she scooped second servings to some people she recognized from church. They thanked her and she smiled. Friends and neighbors laughed and visited under the lights, danced with each other. Still, Mercy wrestled with the deceit and truths of the evening: she had lied about not wanting to change their friendship. It was flat out miserable having life leave her in its wake.

Grabbing an empty pan, Mercy headed to the kitchen. The quietness there allowed her to think without interruption. While she washed the dishes and cried, mentally pondering and debating the endless "what-if's," Kimberly poked her head in.

"Wyatt sent me to check on ya, hon. You alright in here?"

Mercy kept her face to the bubble-filled sink. "Just trying to get a head start."

"Okay, then. Don't stay in here too long. It'll be wrapping up pretty soon."

Kimberly disappeared again, leaving a void and the obvious truth at Mercy's feet. Nothing would change unless she let go of her history, the past she held onto with both hands, as if it could bring Derrick back. She could stay at that sink or move forward.

After wiping her hands dry, Mercy walked back out to the party. Of course, her eyes found Wyatt first. He helped Adele up from her chair, offering his arm to walk her to Heather's truck.

And in the strangest of all notions, Mercy figured out how to ask Wyatt for forgiveness. It was the most bizarre thing she'd ever thought of in her entire life, but it breathed possibility into her scattered mind. Yes, she would have to be brave.

Long after everyone had left, and Mercy had finished with the dishes, she crept toward Wyatt's office. Kimberly mentioned something about him having a headache. Mercy didn't share that his source of pain was none other than herself.

She fought every step toward Wyatt, her head screaming inevitable rejection and her heart pushing her feet forward. Mercy splayed her fingers wide and flexed them into tight fists. It had taken a lot of guts for him to ask her to love him. He'd chosen her over Felicity, despite her insecurities. Now, she needed to have the courage and answer in the only way that made sense to her, the only way that would leave no doubt in his mind either.

He sprawled across the couch, boots shucked and tipped over on the floor. His cowboy hat covered his eyes. The purple blanket wasn't long enough to cover his socks.

Mercy knocked lightly on the door frame. "Wyatt?"

He pushed up the brim of his hat so that his eyes barely showed. "Yeah?"

She took a few steps into the office. "I need to apologize to you." Reaching over, she tugged the blanket to cover his feet.

"Okay." He removed the hat to the floor, perching it upside down.

"I lied, before, when I said that I didn't know how to love and only wanted to be your friend."

Wyatt's leather couch squeaked as he sat up. His jaw worked behind his beard.

"I need to …" Mercy wrung her hands together, terrified of the question she needed to ask. It felt like a sack of flour rested on her chest. "I want to ask you a question, and it's okay if you say no."

"I'm not going to fire you."

Mercy shook her head and stared at the floor. Certainly, he could see her heart racing through the dress, as if it would rip free of her rib cage. "No. I wanted to know if you'll marry me."

There. Her crazy idea fell flat in the now silent room. Knowing Wyatt, he'd still forgive her even if he declined. She could at least say that she tried.

"Wait. What?"

She drove her eyes upward. Wyatt leaned forward onto his knees with both elbows. "You can say no," she whispered. "I understand."

The couch groaned when he stood up, blanket puddling onto the wooden floor. She forced herself to maintain eye contact, fingernails digging into her palms.

His toes banged into hers. "I don't understand. But I don't want to understand right now. Maybe later." He pressed his palms against her cheeks and kissed her deeply. When Mercy pulled back and lowered her head to his chest, he chuckled. Her forehead bounced against his shirt buttons.

"Mercy Benson … my word. If this is how our marriage is getting started, it's going to be an interesting ride."

She grinned into the flannel. "I'll take that as a 'yes.'"

The End

Acknowledgements:

hopes to remember more people this time

Michael. Once again, all of my gratitude and love. You're kinda the best ever.

Dad. You gave me Agatha Christie and didn't even spoil the endings for me. You've shown me how to live a life for the Lord, choosing joy, despite whatever comes.

Mom. You're my example of wisdom and grace. And how to back a horse trailer.

Bean & Squish. Please do that worm dance again.

The best agent ever, Rachel Kent. You keep giving me the reins. It's a blast being your Bookie.

Ashley Mays. You inspire me. Don't stop telling your story. It will be heard.

Robynne. Tell Ian I owe him. Or he owes us. It could go both ways. As long as there are tacos and sarcasm, we're good.

Hannah. Cats and writing. And Sonic blasts.

Rosemary. Just your name. Because I can.

Molly, Lilah, Audrey, and Amelia. Much thanks and love to the time you all took to help me tighten this story.

Vickie. I didn't remember you last time, but the next book has the character named Victoria. Close enough?

Brett Sayles. Your picture inspired me. Thank you for allowing me to share your art with the world.

And the last shall be first. To my savior, Jesus Christ, for giving me these stories. May they honor You.

In case you missed it, please enjoy the first chapter of my novella *True – a contemporary retelling of Rahab*.

Chapter 1

"Put the money on the nightstand."

Maya kept her back to the man when she sat up on the edge of the bed, toes flexing on the cold floor. She shrugged on her silk robe and stood, tying the sash, as her client fumbled with his pants. "Take your time," she said, padding toward the pristine granite and stainless steel kitchen, glancing at the digital clock to check his time. "I will get you a drink."

He seemed like the whiskey type, so she poured a finger into a tumbler. Across the room, the young man sped through the buttons on his shirt, nervously smiling when he saw her watching. "Sorry," he mumbled, jamming the tails into the waist of his designer trousers.

"No need for that. I apologize if I made you feel rushed."

"I should get back to the office, anyways. My boss is breathing down my neck for the border reports."

Maya stepped around the counter and retrieved his tie from the floor. She snaked the blue fabric around his collar and waited until he stilled to begin tying the knot. "It must be awful for you, with the enemy's army a day or two away."

He cleared his throat, looking anywhere but her eyes. "Yeah, a bit nerve-wracking since they rolled over two countries in three months."

"And we are next."

"Looks like it." He grabbed his coat from the chair. "But I shouldn't be talking with you about it."

She helped him settle the jacket onto his shoulders and turned him to work the buttons. Easing a smile across her face, Maya reached up and straightened his hair. "My job is to make you forget, even if for an hour. What you say or do stays in this room."

"Yeah, Henry said that, too."

Maya hummed, and handed him the whiskey, which he knocked back.

"Can I see you again this week?"

"I will send you a text."

"What if I can't make that time?"

She placed her manicured hand on his cheek and raised one eyebrow. The innocence of first-timers always softened her heart a bit. "I'll send you a few options."

He thanked her no less than three times before closing the door. Maya flicked on the doorway cameras and watched him trot down the sidewalk.

After tucking the money into the safe hidden under a bathroom drawer, she changed the linens and reassembled her room before heading to the shower. There was a long three-hour break and she meant to use every minute of it.

Escaping through the opening next to the kitchen, Maya tucked her wet hair into a braid and climbed the stairs to her personal apartment. She slipped through another door and into the heavy overalls and leather apron from the peg next to the door. Metal filings covered the floor. She decided not to sweep until she was done. There were eighty-three more tubes to cut and grind. Then, it was on to assembly.

When her alarm sounded, she was only halfway through. Still, she gathered the materials and headed to the roof. The breeze pushed her sculptures into motion, spinning and reflecting the fading sunlight. Maya deposited the tubes into a pile, each engraved with a number. Soon, they would sing every time the wind blew.

The sun dipped behind the mountain range to the west. Maya looked north, squinting to try and see the invader's camp. Pinprick lights blinked on beyond the river. Only twenty miles of flat farmlands separated them from the capital city, perched on the hill and surrounded by sheer cliffs. It was unsettling—

their previous conquests leveled entire cities from that distance or more. Her house precariously settled inches from the drop-off. Only a few brave men, confronted with their wives banging on the front door, had used her flimsy rope ladder, that lay heaped at the bottom of her rusted red fire escape, to escape down the unclimbable cliff face.

Her second alarm sounded. Ten minutes until General Kohl came for his daily visit. Maya hustled downstairs, fastening the roof hatch behind her. Clean-up would have to wait and she shucked her apron to the floor and pulled on a shimmering robe.

She'd barely dusted her sweat with talc powder and spritzed on the perfume he preferred, when his two-rapped knock sounded at her door. Pulling open the door, Maya smiled wide. "Jared."

"I tried to find your last name again," he said, pushing into her body. "I'll find you out one day."

"A girl has her secrets." And she knew he'd never find her past. She spent her first earnings burying and burning any trace connecting her to the family across town, or the dilapidated house she'd shared with her siblings. No, Jared Kohl would never link Maya to her drunkard father, who was wasting away from cancer. They'd never even seen her beautiful home built on the city cliffs, fortified deep into the bedrock.

Jared buried his lips into her neck, stripping away her robe, all work and no play. "Never underestimate me."

"I never have," she said, stepping backwards to the bed. "That's why you're still allowed to come."

"Less talk."

By the time she redressed, Jared snored deeply. Maya sautéed chicken and vegetables until he stirred. She poured two glasses of wine and plated dinner as he sat on the stool at the counter.

"It's really good," he mumbled between bites.

"I thought I'd try something new. You need more variety in your diet."

"I like meat."

"I know." She sipped her wine and used a nearby remote to close her blinds. "I saw the army earlier, just over the river."

Jared's fork paused near his mouth. "Yeah. The President's sure they won't be able to make it past the defenses."

"He's certainly confident, given their reputation to crush everything in their path." Any city that'd put up a fight was burned to the ground. The news had no shortage of first-hand footage.

"Well, the President's my boss, so I do what he tells me to do." He scraped the fork against the plate. "Got any more?"

Maya served him the last of the stir fry and rinsed her dish. "How many days until they arrive?"

She dried her plate slowly, as if it would delay the army.

"We're sending out an envoy tomorrow, to see if there's any negotiating."

"Are you going?"

Jared snorted. "I'm not that stupid. The last place that tried had their guy's dog tags sent back. Nothing else."

"That's awful." She glanced to the covered windows. "Though it's brilliant psychological warfare."

"And what do you know about that?"

"'The supreme art of war is to subdue the enemy without fighting.'"

"What's that? Something you read?" He jerked his head to her small immaculate bookcase. He had no idea about the one a story above, stretching floor to ceiling, books jammed into every space.

Maya retrieved his plate and dipped it into the suds. "It's Sun Tzu."

"Sun who?" He belched and gulped down the last of his wine.

"Sun Tzu. He wrote 'The Art of War.'"

"Never heard of it."

She kept her eyes on the dish. "He was a Chinese military strategist and writer."

Jared retreated back to the bed and dressed. "Didn't know you were so interested in war."

Refilling his wine, she trailed him and set the glass on the nightstand. "Not war, but in things that are interesting to you. After all, I have to keep you captivated." Though she wanted to strip the bed and start a load of laundry, Maya buttoned Jared's light green work shirt.

He wrapped his soft fingers around her waist. "It's not your brain that interests me."

"Oh? It must be my cooking." Her fingers worked toward the collar.

"No. It's not even the wine."

She patted his chest when he nibbled her shoulder through the expensive robe. "Ah, ah," she said, pulling back. "None of that, General Kohl. You know the rules."

Jared swore. He reached into his pocket and tossed a wad of cash onto her nightstand. "You and your rules."

"Without rules, there is anarchy."

"Sun Tzu?"

"No. Me."

He sat to tie his shoes. "Ah, my mysterious Maya with no last name. Maybe I'll call in a favor to the justice center."

Maya plodded toward the door. She stopped and looked over her shoulder with a practiced smile. "Idle threats."

"No vegetables tomorrow, or I'll do it."

She laughed politely and opened the door. The smile disappeared the moment the lock clicked into place. Skipping his departure on the cameras, Maya cleaned up and showered again. She slipped into some soft pants and a tank top.

Once back inside her workshop with the television news turned on, she swept the metal shavings into a pile while the broadcasters showed the latest footage. The enemy's weapons were more superior than the ones Jared bragged his army had. Even long-range camera shots couldn't hide their infantry numbers. She turned the television off.

The city didn't have a chance.

Maya recycled the filings into a pot to melt. While she worked on the last tubes, she tried not to think about what would happen if the President decided to fight. Instead, she played through scenarios following the city's concession. With no soldiers to pay her way, since they'd surely be pressed into service or jailed, Maya would be left with her art. She could go to the store without worrying about bumping into a client's wife, or having someone mutter, "Slut," as she passed.

But then again, she was quite sure she could fall back on the business she'd built up. Even though the army was rumored to hold to religious, high moral standards, there had to be some in the bunch who craved a woman after a three year-long deployment.

She trudged up the stairs to the roof hatch, trading the smell of singed metal for the damp Delta breeze, cooling off the flat roof of her home. She'd bought the abandoned home because of the view, without a thought of the aging mortar and bricks. Over the last few years, it became her favorite place in the world, as she learned to craft with metal. Solar lights reflected against the sculptures—the spinners twisting next to metal flaps waving from their pegs on a squatted box. The movements reminded her of crows gliding on windy days.

Turning her attention to the towering spindles that looked like a naked, metal tree, Maya stood on her tiptoes to fit the first tube onto the branch. She worked her way across the sculpture, a smile erupting when the fifth tube finally caught the wind and sang. The sixth and seventh hummed in slightly different tones, their sorrowful melody growing and fading depending on the strength of the wind.

Her screwdriver slipped while she was tightening down another branch and Maya sliced her palm against the metal. She hissed and dropped the screwdriver to apply pressure. Abandoning the project, she retreated to her workshop and bandaged her hand, using the first aid kit near the welder. There'd been plenty of times she used the burn ointment and gauze.

Forced to halt her song tree sculpture, Maya plucked a book from her upstairs shelves and settled onto an over-stuffed chair near her single bed covered with a well-used comforter and a red blanket folded near the end. For once, her favorite book couldn't hold her attention. She dimmed the lights and opened the blinds. Across the valley, the lights burned bright at the army's camp. From her window, they almost looked closer than they'd been the day before.

She cranked the window open and pressed her forehead into the screen. She cradled her wounded hand against her chest, drawing in the sweet smell of jasmine that drifted on the air from the tendrils that clung to the building. It reminded Maya of the plant below her mom's kitchen window, with the tiny pink flowers they'd weave into her sister's braids while they dreamed about graduating school and moving out. Maybe they'd get married and become mothers.

Those dreams died years before.

A pounding on the door below made Maya slam her hand on the window frame and stinging pain zipped up her arm. No one had made an appointment. She walked down to the monitors near the door and watched the man sway on his feet before placing a hand on the wall to steady himself. He battered on the steel again.

"Can I help you?" Maya used the intercom she had installed to keep the drunks away.

The man leaned into the peephole, as if it were the microphone. "Jared said … Jared sent me."

"I'm sorry, but I am not able to see you right now. If you leave a card, I can contact you."

"No, I need to come in now." He banged his fist on the door.

"I do apologize, but you'll need to leave before I call the patrol."

"I am the patrol." A clumsy hand shoved a badge at the peephole and it scraped into the metal.

"Please, leave me your card and we can work something out."

His foot met the kickplate several times. "Let me in. I have money."

Maya sighed and sent a message to the city patrolmen. Sure, this one would be embarrassed, but it wouldn't be the first one she'd called coworkers to lead away one of their own. "It doesn't work that way."

He snarled insults into the night. She watched as he paced, then stumbled across the street. A couple of his colleagues arrived and guided him down the sidewalk.

With a yawn, Maya went back upstairs and curled onto the small bed to sleep, pulling the soft red blanket over her clothes. The jasmine wandered through her memories until she fell asleep.

When someone pounded on the door again, Maya was sure the drunk was back. Cracking her eyelids open, sunlight marched in through the open window and directly into her eyes. The second thumping was more insistent as she descended. She swept her hair into a bun when she saw Jared on the monitors.

"General Kohl," she said, opening the door. "Is everything all right?"

"No." He shoved past her and marched straight to the window. "Their army isn't advancing, and they fired warning shots when our ambassadors approached."

"Oh my." Her practiced words covered the panic in her mind. Without some type of negotiations, they wouldn't survive. Everything she'd worked for would be for nothing.

"The city will be put into curfew before dark. There will be a patrol checkpoint on the road in and no one gets in or out." Jared closed the window and clicked the remote to close the curtains. "So, I won't be by later. Keep your monitors on. Rumor has it that they will try and send in spies to scope out our defenses."

"Will you be safe?"

His eyes closed and he scrubbed the thin hair just above his wrinkled forehead. "I'll be next to the President, trying to figure out how to make it out of this. You have enough food?"

It was the first time Jared had offered kindness rather than money.

"I do, thank you."

"Keep your door bolted and call me if someone shows up."

Maya nodded.

"Here." He reached into his pocket and pressed some bills into her hand. "Don't let anyone in."

She barely tipped her lips up and nodded again, feeling as cheap as the unsolicited, rumpled money in her fist. The lock slid into place and she dropped the payment near the door.

In her workroom, Maya turned on quiet music. She knew the radio and television would be blasting panic and simultaneous presidential rhetoric, neither of which she wanted to hear. After a couple hours of cleaning and rearranging materials, Maya returned to her rooftop project.

She felt like a vampire in the sun with the normal evening hours she kept for clients, but worked in a wide sunhat and gloves. When her arms felt floppy from placing the tubes in a cascading, circular pattern, she stood and stretched. Her body ached more than it should for her age. Her stomach rumbled. The wind sang through the different tubes, all around the hollow trunk as she fastened the roof hatch.

After eating over the sink, Maya popped a couple of aspirin and slathered lotion on her angry, pink sunburn. Clients paid for smooth skin, not peeling blotches. She retrieved the book from the night before and slid onto the cool tiled floor near the kitchen to soothe her skin. Mr. Darcy had snubbed Elizabeth Bennet when a quiet knock came at her door.

Through the monitors, two men looked down the nearly empty street, then whispered to one another. Their skin was dark from the sun and their pants too clean and new. One knocked softly again, before quietly asking, "Hello?" The tourist caps emblazoned with a city name a few hours north were slung low across their eyes. The city had been razed weeks before.

The hairs on the back of Maya's neck pricked.

These were the spies.

She pulled her phone from her pocket and brought up Jared's number. Something brushed against her bare foot—Jared's cash. Rumpled singles that he probably used for some seedy club across town with the boys.

Maya twisted the lock and opened the door. "Please, come in before you are seen."

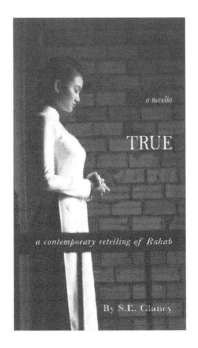

"*True* – a contemporary retelling of Rahab"
Available in paperback and e-book on
Amazon.

Also by S.E. Clancy:

"Encircled"

Experience six of the world's most beloved stories in a whole new light! From historical to futuristic, these retellings will take you to an enchanted forest, a cursed castle, and far beyond. Uncover secrets of a forbidden basement, a hypnotic gift, and a mysterious doll. Fall in love with a lifelong friend or brand-new crush. Venture to unknown lands on a quest to save a prince, a kingdom, or maybe even a planet. With moments of humor, suspense, romance, and adventure, *Encircled* has something to offer every fan of fairy tales, both classic and reimagined.

~

Come join in on the shenanigans! Follow me at:

seclancy.com

Instagram: authorseclancy

Facebook: Author S.E. Clancy

Made in the USA
Lexington, KY
23 November 2019

57535159R00074